Thursdays in the Rain
An urban horror collection

Jennifer Rachel Baumer

Monstrosity Ink

Reno, Nevada

Thursdays in the Rain
An urban horror collection

Monstrosity Ink

Contents

Some questions should never be answered.

Blood Kiss

Sister Alice Shooting Star walks down to the corner store, looking for change, hey, any spare change, sir? And a pack of Marlboros and a Diet Coke. She's tall and rangy, head like a recently harvested corn field, all white yellow and spiky. No one bothers her here on the street. Dark day. Coastal muggy; the palms look ragged and winterdead. The streets are rotting and the sidewalks smell, patchwork and polka dots of cracks and filth. There are beggars in her path, more apt than she at caging change.

The store front screams tired desperation. The Korean behind the counter gives her a tightlipped greeting that betrays the pump action shotgun under the counter but Sister Alice Shooting Star comes neither to steal nor rob. She has made two dollars and seventeen cents on the way here, $1900 at the airport from a group of inveterate and guilty gamblers returning from a junket to Reno. Sister Alice wants only what she has come for; smokes and drinks before she returns to the convent. Guru Mitashi waits, his fists coiled in displeasure sharp as a wasp's sting, and she believes in discipline, believes in towing the line and worship and faith. She believes Mitashi has been sent to show them the way, but she misses the times that came before. Once punishment was work and Sister Alice learned from her misdeeds (always unexpected, one day she was to peel the apples, the next they were sacred and untouchable) and then punishment was corporal, the thud of a fist or crack of a cat against her skin and even then she understood and learned the error of her ways (the proper ways to please her master and when devotionals were to be performed and the cooking of the sacrificial rice and ham).

Now things have changed and punishment is unpredictable, the kiss of a needle against her neck, locked in the steam room while inhalants pump through the vents, time spent in isolation with a steady drip of chemicals in her veins, out of her mind in terror and her guru's voice leading her journeys of discovery and overarching fear. For an instant she thinks about not returning. She has the money. She hasn't gone back to the convent yet. How far could she run on $1900? The other side of the country? Or straight up, north to Seattle and from there into Canada, leave the rest of them behind?

But she can't. Mouse with his gray eyes and tiny, sad mouth, Robin quick wit and beaten eyes, and Davy, sinking every day into slavery.

She pays for the smokes. She had not meant to think the word slavery. She believes. She is a good girl, a nun. She is pure, untouched except where the master's hands have had her, where the brands stand out and the scarification and now she is on the street and her steps lead her away away free of that life and onward and upward and she drops the red and white pack of Marlboros along the way. She has been shredding them as she goes. The sun is in her eyes, she's heading north and west and the commune is south and east, convent, okay, and Sister Alice Shooting Star comes to a gate she never realized was there, as if her city lives within a city, as if her reality lives trapped within someone else's and she knocks tentatively on the gate to see what will happen. She is hours late in returning already. She will be severely punished, speedball, STP, evil psychedelics and the master death tripping her, she may as well reward her curiosity before turning back.

The gate is set high in a tall stone and iron fence. The fence stretches in either direction as far as she can see. And she stands, Sister Alice, and waits, and the gate opens.

"Welcome."

He takes her hand. Treats her like an invalid, an escapee, treats her like a refuge or guest. Treats her like a prisoner. His hands are soft on her arms but when she twists in his grip for one last look at the street behind her the hands tighten until she cries, head forced forward. The gate slams closed and the women come for her, priestesses, nuns of some other religion, adherents of some other master. She is born into the temple, stripped clean and washed. She cries, thinking they mean to sacrifice her, they men to take her back. The women lead her, altar steps, a board to lay on, face down and uncomfortable and afraid and she feels the knife beginning to work on her back, new patterns growing high and sharp and ridged over the old and with every slash and sting and slip of the knife the door in front of her opens wider, sunlit path to freedom and Sister Alice Shooting Star waits for her release.

***

A week since the door swung open and freedom was at hand, and the patterns on his back have infected. Virus has settled into his bones; his blood burns with it. Mouse sits huddled against rock, blanketed only by stone and plant. He came looking for Alice and he thought she'd led the way. He'd followed the trail of broken cigarettes and torn and shredded filters, she was always the one after the master to stop smoking. Show them the way and lead them not into temptation and death. But when Mouse reached the gate where the cigarette trail led it was into another form of slavery and betrayal. Alice had gone on without him and he could no longer go back, slipped away from the convent without telling anyone and without asking, the dregs of a bad MDA trip still raging through him, nausea and fear and headache. When the gate opened he went through it and when they took him to the altar he didn't fight but lay as they arranged him and endured the knives making mockery of his flesh until it ended. When they let him go he picked up the trail again, imagined he followed her by the sickly sweet scent of her own infected wounds until he realized he smelled himself and then he went to ground, huddling and afraid.

The world around him was bleak, different from what he knew and loved, from the fear-filled city he had left, warm nights fuck-me-in-the-garden moons and high school dating until Mitashi had come along, promising answers to questions in the City of Answers, questions Mouse didn't even know he had, and when he realized where he was, how lost and far from home, mother and father dead, burned to death in a fire that took their pedestrian, middle aged, middle class house, when it was too late Mouse realized he wanted to run and that's when Mitashi pulled him back, laced him up with PCP and left him suspended for three days, screaming and vomiting and going up and coming down until Alice intervened on his behalf.

And Mouse fell in love.

He surfaces and faces again the fact she ran, she fucking ran and left him here and Mouse bites the inside of his cheek until it bleeds and knows what he will do to her once he finds her. Hands clench. Teeth grit. Blood flows in his mouth. The sickly flower sweet smell of rot goes with him when he goes looking for her again. Another three days, no food for two, no water for one and Mouse falls. His feet beat a virus dance against the desert floor. As if it were an SOS, she answers.

Golden hair, longer now, impossible it could have grown so quickly.

Radiant eyes. Her wounds smell but not like his. He has found her, alive and whole, or she has found him. Anger flies, he cannot harm her, she is his love, twin soul, the one he had to find of all that have left the master.

He reaches out to her and that's when he sees the knife in her hand and understands that she has been searching for him, too. At first he shrinks back from her, from the knife, and Sister Alice frowns at him, then looks to the knife and laughs. She throws it into the bushes and takes his hand.

The broken cigarettes have washed away. There's no sign of them now on the gray and broken sidewalks. No way of knowing how long they've been inside the gates. Days and nights blurred together. Alice stayed outside with Mouse the night after they found each other. He couldn't move or travel, couldn't even be carried and even stick thin as he'd become, Sister Alice couldn't carry him. In the end, he'd only gotten to the wilds of the yard of the imposing Victorian with the iron fence and the high enclosing gate. Fever burned him. His skin was hot enough to warm her while he shivered and shook. She tried to hold him, tried to clean the wounds on his back. At last she packed the designs with grass, not knowing what else to do. Plain old ordinary grass that shouldn't have been able to do anything but stick in the blood and turn his skin lightly green. So maybe it was the touch of her hands that healed him but by morning the fevers had passed and the wounds smelled distant and not so rank.

Morning wakes them, greasy sky with a faint glow of sun beneath it. Gas station bathroom. She uses handfuls of brown recycled paper towels to clean him, terrified she'll reignite his back. Mouse presses against her ministrations – he's healing ant it itches. They giggle like children and she shows him the money. The Victorian place, they didn't care about money, never asked. She hasn't been back to the convent.

They eat breakfast at a buffet. "As much food as you can safely eat before your starved, abused body rejects it" the sign should have read but it just reads "all you can eat" and they do, filling paper napkin doggie bags when no one is looking with ham and cookies and grapes. They eat the cookies on the way to the mall, new clothes, new haircuts, new day and now to the bus station, one way tickets back to Alice's home town, call to her mother before and yes, yes, anything, yes, bring the boy but come home, baby, there are no questions, no answers, just come home.

Tickets in hand. How long till take off? Small game rooms but Ms Packman is too old. Outside in the sun, talking lazily about the convent and,

"Pretty."

"Excuse me?"

"I'm sorry, that was forward. I said you are pretty."

"Thank you," but Sister Alice Shooting Star is frowning. The guy looks like a businessman, all tie and suit, briefcase and cell phone. Anyone can have those things, of course.

"You've been hurt," he says. He includes Mouse in the statement but it's Sister Alice he's looking at. "Someone has hurt you."

She doesn't know what to say to him. She doesn't need money, not right now. It's been a long time since a stranger has shown concern simply because Alice has been hurt. Confused, she glances at her watch instead of answering but the bus is still hours away.

"Let me help you," the businessman says and Mouse is looking at him. As if the man can actually do something for them.

"How?" Her voice grates harsh as a crows' speak. She wants to break his hold on Mouse. "We've eaten. We have money. We're all right." Go away. "We're going home."

The businessman purses his lips. "Without the answers you came to find. Such a shame. To leave the city without the answers."

A crow is startled into laughter at this; it arches overhead, black sail against sunlight.

"That's what you came here for, isn't it? Answers?"

Mouse is rapt. He wouldn't hear Alice if she spoke. He wouldn't come with her if she dragged him. And they're even now, aren't they? He saved her life and she saved his. Or has she saved his twice? She can't remember. Either way she can give him the ticket to get a refund, she can go home alone.

But it doesn't work that way. Mouse is in her blood, his confusion, his longing. She'll go on seeing him forever poised at the door of the businessman's black 325i BMW, that look of longing on his face.

One last time. "Mouse, please let's go back inside the station."

But he doesn't even look at her, into the car and he gets in the back so she can get in the front because Alice gets carsick and the only thing she can do is follow.

A hand knocks her to her knees. Other hands press a prayerbook into hers. The floor under her knees is cement. She hasn't eaten or seen Mouse in two days, not since the businessman brought them here. Sister Alice's hair is limp and dirty. Her clothes smell again. The cuts on her back have begun to fester in the heat of the cell. When she moves they break open, trailing hot blood down her back.

"Prayer," they told her. "It will open doors."

But the door remains locked.

"It will answer questions."

She has forgotten the questions.

"It will fill you up. It will make you whole. You will come to crave it."

But she cannot crave something she never stops doing. She prays night and day. They wake her. They berate her. They force her trembling back to her knees.

At least she can remember the questions again, she thinks in the endless moments between consciousness and loss. She is a good girl. She does not understand. She doesn't know if she should fight.

***

Mouse comes for her eventually. Third day or maybe fourth. His back has healed and he has found the reserves of strength from somewhere to force his way past the chaste and holy who come to give him water. He has discovered his cell is nothing more than a hall closet with locks. He has released three others on his way to finding Sister Alice in her basement cell. He is thin and beaten but he takes her hand and pulls her up and when she shivers against him in fever, he holds her tight and gives her his strength.

They have lost their money (seekers of the way do not need money, they were told, and true, within the confines of the cell they had no use for it). They have lost their clothes (the faithful dress in rags, they are told, though those who tended them seemed finely dressed). They have lost their bus tickets, unredeemable at this late date anyway. Sister Alice still wears her watch. She can sell that.

Mouse just looks puzzled and lost. "Can you make it?" he asks. They'll have to walk.

"With you," she tells him.

She's waiting for them when they get off the bus. City bus, transfer point. They're still in the City of Answers. Late evening and dirty rain, city rain falling but she doesn't look drenched, doesn't even look wet. She crooks a finger – *follow me* – to lead them to the waiting limo. Inside there's food and heat and light, all the things they've been doing without. Whippet thin, girl and boy, the girl's cornfield hair just long enough to start turning to dreads. Heroin chic cheekbones. They have the swollen mouths of onlookers at a feast and it's not until she urges them – *go ahead, this is for you* – that they dig in, hungry mouths and greasy fingers and eyes never leaving the food, as if afraid they will wake and find themselves praying in closets or stretched upon an altar or begging in an airport or starving to the dripfeed of the master's chemicals. When she gives them the command, they don't even respond the first time, just continue their gluttony, satiating the hunger inside them. But she wants them hungry, wants them wanting, and the second time she speaks the girl lays a hand on the boy's arm, stopping him mid-bite, food falling away from his face. The girl is still trying to find her way. Still searching for purity within herself. She's a good girl, still searching for answers – even while looking for a way home.

The Queen of Knives hands him a blade, razor-handled, and nods. This is the reason she brought them (or bought them). This is the payment they must make, not paid in full but promising payment before she'll take them any further. Before she'll Answer any Questions.

The boy looks reluctant. The girl moves first, face lost and lonely, streethaunted. She raises her shirt, slips her arms free, tugs it over her head and sits shivering, despite the heat in the car. Mouse throws the Queen a look between desperation and despair and fear, reluctance in every twitch, every blink, and she slowly, almost imperceptibly, nods.

He moves slowly. Maybe that makes it worse. Maybe it makes it better. He draws the blade along Sister Alice's breast, thin red line following and filling until blood flows down pale flesh and drips from the nipple. Only then does the Queen relent, leaning forward to catch the blood on her tongue, then upward to Alice's lips, bloody tongue against innocent tongue and into her mouth breathes, "Eat of my flesh," and Alice replies, "Drink of my blood."

The Queen draws back and nods at Mouse. "again." But his mouth is full of Alice's blood, his eyes are full of Alice. He fell in love with her before and now he sees her lost and scarred before him.

"No."

The Queen's eyes fill with rage. "Again. You came looking for answers. We will find them. Again." She reaches out, perhaps to press Mouse's hand down into Alice's breast, the hand holding the wood-handled razor and that hand rises, smoothly, of its own accord, as if answering its own questions and presses against the Queen's neck

"Put your clothes back on," he tells Alice, who has gone still and wary, and then, "Get the food. And our money."

The Queen spits at him, and misses. Spittle dots the upholstery of the limo. Alice rummages through the collection box the woman has attached to the bar in the long car. "There's more," she says.

"Take it." He doesn't waver with the razor and when Alice has everything packed, he sends her out of the car and backs out after her. They stand watching, afraid to turn their backs and walk away. What happens next? But the limo simply slides into gear and accelerates and disappears into the city.

They stand watching as the limo pulls away and finally Alice says softly, "Who am I? Why am I here? Will anyone ever love me for more than what I can give to them?"

"Sister Alice Shooting Star," Mouse says, and takes her hand. "Second answer, to get on a bus. To go home. To start over." He looks down at her. He looks younger when he smiles. "Third answer: someone already does."

She stands still, watching him, as if trying to believe the answers can be that simple. Trying to understand that there can be answers, that she could be someone's answer. When Mouse smiles she takes his hand and points them both in the direction of the bus station.

Fugue State started with a dream — someone else's. My friend Aynjel told me about a
nightmare she'd had with shadows that moved about in corners and made chittering
sounds. The image haunted me for days, until finally it ended up in
a rather nightmarish story.

Fugue State

There are shadows in this house.

Turn a light on. .

That would be my husband Dean, if he were home. He's not, at the moment, I don't know where he is and I don't care, but it doesn't matter: I can read his mind.

Not that way. I'm not psychic and I'm not crazy. I just know the way he thinks, the things he says.

And turning a light on wouldn't help. They're not those kinds of shadows. These shadows chitter, and hurry. They make sounds I cannot bear and they gather in the sunlight.

I cannot say this to Dean. I would be the recipient of one of his looks, both condescending and agonized and then God help me he would help me. I cannot bear that.

After all, I am only here because of Dean.

Or to put it another way, the only reason I'm here is Dean.

He's never hurt me physically — at least, I don't think he has, though time will tell with some of what he's done. The experimental drugs. The experimental therapy. I married him because it was the only way out. Had I not agreed, my records would still say I was hopelessly insane (we don't use that word here — yes, you do) and recommend continued hospitalization and the chief of staff's recommendations are seldom ignored.

I can't argue with him because while he may never have hurt me physically,   he's   hurt   me   in   so   many   creative   ways.

The first time I saw them I'd only been "home" less than a week. Home from that whole "whirlwind courtship" everyone thought was so romantic and wonderful, the recovered patient, the caring doctor, the unexpected and possibly unethical romance, but who cares about ethics when they're both so beautiful and the story is so sweet?

It *was* a whirlwind. The sudden recovery, drug dosages dropping off like pounds on an Atkins' diet. Like snowstorms in spring. The world kept getting clearer and brighter every day and I didn't understand what was happening and then suddenly I did and that was worse. Because when insanity washed away and reality came in like high tide, I found that stuffy, too-warm darkness in my head had been better.

Whirlwind proposal (*you will*). Plans (*we shall*). Wedding (*she does, you do*). Honeymoon (*it is*). Home (*welcome, honey, disturb nothing*).

Disturb nothing. I was already disturbed enough.

I saw the first shadow the first week. Maybe the second. It seems likely I had at least a week in the sunlight before he started my "therapy."

Dusty haze. The skin on my forehead felt thick and numb. I'd have rubbed it if I could have but wrapped away in a cocoon of Thorazine it was all I could do to move from room to room in that house, following the sun as it trekked across the late autumn sky. Thorazine is like viewing an impressionist world while wrapped snugly and too tightly in a warm, wet army blanket. Something in it seems to separate the sides of the brain. When you walk, same arm/same leg swing together and you feel like you're falling. When you think, thoughts seem unable to bridge the gap between lobes. Sides. Whatever. That's his territory, not mine. My brain is his territory, not mine. I am no longer so familiar with it.

There are shadows in this house.

Turn a light on.

I'm afraid to.

I don't want to see what's there.

Laura spent the day with June. Just being out of the house was a gift, being with Juney again, but Dean had added to it that morning when he handed her a credit card and told her she could paint her office any color she chose and he didn't give her any psychological insights on what colors might mean. He'd given her a kiss as June honked from the driveway and they were off.

"That's the biggest cup of coffee I've ever seen," June said. "Are you thinking of drowning yourself?"

Just for an instant Laura blinked at the suggestion of suicide, self-harm, instability, and then she grinned. "Dean doesn't approve of coffee."

June blinked across the tiny round table at her. "So, what, he doesn't allow you to have it?" She poured the contents of four packets of sweetener into her small cup.

Laura raised her eyebrows. June frowned with mock severity. "We're discussing your foibles, not mine."

"Foibles?"

"If you let your husband decide on your coffee drinking and then try to make up for lost time. Honestly, that's Big Gulp size."

It was, and Laura was happy with it, and June's teasing and the mall and the pale peach paint she'd bought and arranged to have delivered. She was happy enough to dissemble a bit for Dean's sake.

"He has a whole cupboard filled with teas I like. I don't want to hurt his feelings." But she finished the titanic-sized coffee and June nodded and kept her thoughts to herself and outwardly the day was glorious.

She did not think about going home to the shadow-filled house.

"Call me if you need me," June had said just before Laura got out of her car. But that sounded like Laura was in some kind of danger. Of course she wasn't. She was home.

She woke calmly, with pleasure. Warm under the covers, she remembered it was Saturday. Dean had rounds at the county hospital today. If she was lucky she'd have till early afternoon alone in the house. No Dean. No questions. No answers.

Laura opened her eyes and frowned. Shadows. There would be shadows. The thought drove her upright in the bed. Bright sunlight streaked over Dean's polished hardwood floors. Crystals in the window sent rainbows flying. The house was warm and she could smell toast from downstairs. After 9:00, according to the clock radio. June would be up by now, easily. She could call, arrange brunch, be off to meet her before Dean could even think of leaving the hospital and then a movie – can't have your cell on in a movie after all, and –

A shadow, fat and thick as a raccoon, slid across the floor. The movement suggested too many legs, something like a centipede. Something *hurrying*.

From long practice, Laura bit back a scream. She gasped, then moaned once. One hand came up and covered her mouth. Then Dean was in the doorway, face concerned, all the professional demeanor gone: his face was a mix of concern (for his poor wife) and exasperation (over his annoying wife.) "What'd you see?"

Nothing. *Nothing.*

"I . . . was dreaming." She refused to look back at the floor. She watched him.

"You were sitting up," he said without emphasis. That was worse. Calm sometimes meant trouble. The Doctor Is In. You didn't want the doctor to be in.

She shook her head. From the corner of her eye she could see the unmarked sunny wood floor. "I was dreaming," she repeated.

"About what?" His voice was deliberate. Slow.

About you. Tell him about you. *Something happened to you. He'll be flattered.* "I dreamed something happened to you." And this was treacherous, too. Who would hurt him; why? Not to mention the patients at the hospital. Not to threaten or imply they didn't adore him. Not to suggest anyone could mean him harm.

Definitely not to remind him she'd been a patient.

"I dreamed you leaned over to kiss me," she said and met his eyes. "I sat up to kiss you back."

For an instant he had no expression, and then he smiled, a dark-haired man with dark eyes standing at the edge of their bedroom. "Then I should." He crossed to her, scattering rainbows on the way. She watched him until he was close, then shut her eyes and turned her face up to his.

Sometimes, like this, it was almost all right. Sometimes, when he was like this, she could believe he loved her.

"I got Lucille to take my shift today. She owed me from when she was having that affair and I had to keep covering for her long, long lunches and early outs and disappearances."

Lucille. Dr. Tarron. Aggressive, unsympathetic, more of the Nazi camp than behaviorist or Freudian. Dr. Tarron was taking Dean's place. *Lucky patients,* Laura thought wistfully. Still, it wasn't so bad right at this moment. One of Dean's hands caressed her shoulder where she lay across his chest. Laura stared, eyes unfocused, into the moving sun lighting the bedroom. "If I wanted to, I could probably never go in again she owes me so much time."

Something moved. A shadow. No, several of them. Sliding up the wall near the corner of the bedroom, just beyond the windows, just past the sunlight. A column of shadows that danced and flickered like something alive, as if it heard what Dean had said, flown up that instant to fill the corner because he'd said "I could stay home every day with you."

Lightly. Pleasantly. Turning his head to kiss her lips and *don't let him see, don't let him see, don't let him know that I've seen something* –

But she saw the look in his eyes, and it was already too late.

The bath water swirls around her, warm, almost too warm. The drugs make her drowsy and he won't tell her what he's given her. Laura keeps her head up by force of will, staring around the bathroom as if she's never seen it before. Every feature, catalogued. Every nook and cranny, every fleck of misplaced paint or bruise of wallpaper. Anything she can concentrate on to keep herself awake. Aware. She's too dependent on him now. He's wrapped her in warm wet sheets, so close and tight, a cocoon of wet warmth even before he lowered her into the hot bath. The drugs in her system swirl through her, dizzying. She wishes she knew what to expect. The dizzy, dry-mouthed confusion of Thorazine. The spacey, sad, displaced dissociation of Demerol. Nightmare-wracked barbiturates. The occasional terror of hallucinogens.

The worst part, though. Not the drugs. Not the confinement. Not the clammy wet of sheets against her skin in a water bath or the fear he'd walk away and she'd slide down and drown. The worst part was him sitting on the edge of the tub, brushing the wet tendrils away from her flushed wet face, his calm voice the voice of the doctor who wants to help and understand and fix.

"What did you see? Laura, what did you think you saw? I need you to confide in me. You need to understand there's nothing there. Together we can figure this out. I can help you, Laura, help you understand what the hallucinations mean and then together we can make them stop. We can exorcize the demons but you have to trust me. You have to trust me and let me help you."

His voice was unending, a cadence underscored by her slow droning heartbeat.

Please let me go.

Above the tub several shadows rushed together on the vacant wall. He wasn't watching her so she let her eyes rest on them, following their movement. She couldn't block his voice. He talked, reassuring, calming. Loving. About her misapprehensions and fears and hallucinations. About helping her so she'd never see them again, so she could be healthy.

The shadows poised above the bath tub, clearly visible to her. She wasn't afraid of them now. They seemed to offer strength. If Dean did not want her to see them, they must be something right, and good. Something she didn't want sent away.

"I can help you, damn it," Dean said, because she wasn't listening. "Do you always want to be this way?"

Why not? Laura wondered, the drugs pulling away from her as she watched the shadows cavort. After all, she wasn't crazy.

I'm not crazy.

I'm not crazy. I was. When my first husband died, so soon after the wedding, when I found myself alone in the home we'd planned for two. Then, yes. Then I found an escape hatch and I took it, fled to it and people who cared about me found me, not eating, not sleeping, not bathing or coping. Not sane. I hurt all over then and it didn't matter to me what they did. My parents were gone, years ago, my sister a distant stranger who lived across the country. There was June, my best friend, and other friends, but that hadn't been enough to hold me. A guardian was appointed. The house was sold, our possessions put into storage and in a way, I was put into storage also. It's not that no one at state cared if any of us got better. No one was actually mean or criminally unconcerned. It was just so understaffed, so few of them and so many of us and my sad little story didn't leave them much to work with until Dean came along.

Dean pulled me out of myself. He made me laugh. He listened. What I didn't know was how he was manipulating my drugs, the dosages he raised and lowered so I felt better when he was around, more thick and sad and lost when he was gone. By the time I figured it out it was far too late; wedding preparations were underway and the only way I was getting out now was by marrying my doctor and the only place I had to go was here.

Where the shadows are.

He releases me long after the bath has gone cold. He rubs my back and helps me get dressed. I hang on to him as he walks me to the kitchen, as stumbling and weak as a newborn kitten. He fixes me eggs and sits across from me while I try to eat. There's no point fighting. The eggs make me sick after the drugs but when I refused to eat once he intubated me, forced food directly into my stomach, doctor's orders, you need to keep up your strength. When I fought the restraints, he wrapped me so tight the sheets bruised and burned. When I fought him he drugged me for so many days I no longer knew who or where I was.

He   doesn't   understand   the   fight   has   only   changed.

There is no point in fighting the eggs. I eat them and drink the putrid floral cup of Earl Grey he pours me. I nibble toast, which at least is comforting to my stomach. I wait for the analysis that comes with the food.

"Laura, look at me."

The late morning sun is in my eyes. Dean is only a dark shape looming across the table from me. This seems right. I don't squint or strain to see better. The sun behind his black form creates a field of white around him. He glows. As if he's holy.

"Laura, these things you think you see. You know what they are, don't you? You understand what it truly is you're seeing?"

Everything in me stiffens, trying to remember. Has he told me this theory before?

Fortunately, he doesn't wait for me to answer. "It's just memory, love. Sadness. You've been through so much. The shadows, they're just representations of what you've lost, things you're not ready to face."

I take another bite of toast. Reasonable, I suppose, if rather blatantly obvious. It would even make sense if the shadows were more figurative, less literal. More ambiguous, less solid. It would make sense if only they didn't speak. If only I didn't understand them.

His voice becomes strained. "Laura, look at me."

I squint into the light now, past him. The sun has moved a little, still blinding in this tiny kitchen, and I can see the shadows gathering past him. Something in his voice has changed. I take another bite of toast, suddenly afraid again, and "Put down the toast," he says.

"You said I should eat." I reach for the tea, toast wedge still in the other hand. Dean bangs his hand down on the table and the silver rattles and jumps, the tea spills.

"I said you should *trust* me," he says. Shadows stir behind him, agitated, chittering. It takes all my will power not to look at them. I'm positive he can hear them. My heart pounds. Sweat breaks down my spine. I'm so afraid. June's known something's wrong, known for a while. If I can distract him and get out, go to June's, hide –

"Don't you want to be free?" he asks, his voice too velvet over raggedness. "Don't you want to exorcize your demons?"

Behind him the shadows boil up, raging, tearing at each other. He twitches, one hand brushing back behind him. He hears them, but he won't admit it.

"Put down the toast! You need my help! I have to help you!"

Help   *us!*

Their voices are clear now. I've never been afraid of them. For all that I've been afraid of practically everything since Dean brought me here, I've never been afraid of the shadows.

Across from me Dean breaks off, his face blank for an instant, then full of rage. He shoots up from his seat, both hands smashing down on the table even as he leans across it toward me.

"What do you know? How much? How long?"

I take a step away. I'm still so weak from the drugs, the bath, everything he's done to me. Like he's split me into a hundred little pieces, always telling me he wants to help, always shattering anything that threatens to be whole.

Until there'll be nothing left of me but a shadow.

I stop, then, staring at him, and the voices come through more clearly than ever, individual voices, men and women and somewhere in there, a child.

"How could you?" I ask. I've stopped moving, no longer retreating. Dean still comes toward me but his steps are uncertain. He looks past me and I don't have to turn: I can feel them gathering close to me, remnants; pieces, only.

"I had to." He spreads his hands, reasonable, explaining. Explaining even though a *doctor* certainly doesn't owe an explanation to a *patient*. "It's my calling. I'm a doctor. I have to help them save themselves. Help them exorcize their demons."

"You've haven't done that great a job, have you?" Furious, now, as the adrenaline starts flushing the drugs from my system. I'm sweating, as if the poison is sliding off my skin. "What about all the ones who went out and *did* things? The ones who killed and raped and . . . and *did* things, *after* they'd been treated by the great Doctor Grace?"

. . . Two nurses, in my room. I'm recovering, but slowly, bits and pieces of myself coming back to me and Dean has asked me to marry him and the staff is consumed with it, the congratulations, the questions, the jokes, the well wishes, all of it within his earshot. But he's not here right now, and me? I'm catatonic again. Cataleptic. Shocky. *Gone.* They can say anything they want around me.

. . . Two nurses, in my room. A hushed but nasty little conversation.

"The Amazing Grace," one says, emptying some container into another. Today my eyes don't want to track. I sit in the wheelchair and stare out the window and the nurses keep talking.

"At   least   she   won't   be   like   the   others."

"It's not all of them," says the younger, smaller nurse. Probably she's been dazzled by him; he's beautiful, Dr. Dean Grace, in the same way a sleek, overly-expensive car is beautiful. You may desire it, see yourself going really fast in it, but you know it will never love you, never give anything back, never fit easily in your garage.

The older nurse doesn't even glance my way. "No, not all of them, or even those idiots on the review board would figure out something's wrong. But too many of his've gone rogue. Come in for torturing animals and gone out to kill humans. It's like instead of making them better, he's making them better at doing it. 'Stead of taking out the bad . . ."

The little nurse makes a sound, a jolted motion, and the older nurse breaks off. Dean stands in the doorway, staring at me like nothing else exists, but did he hear them? Did I ever see either of those nurses again?

"It's like instead of taking out the bad . . ."

"He's taking out the good," I say aloud, and look directly at him. Exorcizing the demons . . . or casting out the good.

It's a huge leap in logic.

It makes no sense.

It's magical thinking of the worst kind. Any doctor worth his salt would have me back on meds in an instant.

It's right. I can see it in his face. The hatred and rage, the angry little boy caught playing with matches or beating the neighbor's dog with a stick. It's not a question anymore – from conjecture to knowledge in one hateful glance.

I'm trapped. My legs barely hold me standing. I only got as far as the kitchen with Dean's help. The adrenaline is making my heart race and making me dizzy but I'm no more able to run than I was before.

You bitch. You whore. What do you know? How can you?

But I can't hear him. My ears are screaming with shock and adrenaline, buzzing, ringing, full of the voices around me.

Weak voices. Lost voices. The good sides of his patients, their anger and violence removed . . . set free. They are shadows.

I take another step back and stumble over something, a chair maybe. Dean's black medical bag maybe. It catches the back of my calf, my arms start to reach, *I'm falling!* but it's Dean reaching to save me so I let go, go soft as the drugs would have me, fall into the mass of chittering, hurrying shadows.

Weightless. Floating. This is a void. Was I afraid of dying? This is nothing. Not fear or pain. I just . . . am.

From somewhere I can hear them. I've said I was never afraid of them but is that true? They're all around me. Soft as cats, they drift against me with no real sense of touch. Am I the same? Soft, formless– a shadow. A thrill of fear runs through me. I can still feel that at least. This is not the release I've wanted. I am trapped here. I am *nothing* here.

Help us.

How?

Amorphous shapes. Histories. Lives. A sense of stories passed, missed opportunities, longed for events. Stories. They're stories. No. They're more than that. They're ghosts, the remains Dean left behind. The good parts he had no use for.

It's like 'stead of taking out the bad, he took out the good.

Bodies, exorcized, out there worse than they had been. The killings. The rapes. The indescribable anger and violence. A few more and even those idiots on the review board would have noticed. A few more.

MY body is out there. Whatever I am, however lost I've become, part of me remains with Dean. The angry parts. The violent bits. The part that fought him when he took me from state, the part that twisted and thrashed and gave him a black eye before screaming off on foot, stopped such a short distance later when the drugs made me too slow.

Not this time. This time he won't feed me – what's left of me – drugs. He won't want me incapacitated.

All you have to do is wait.

All I have to do is wait.

And send a piece of myself back.

He'll want me aware.

But he didn't. And the needle closed in. And the world was closed out.

Impressions only. Jagged flashes of awareness. Dean, above her, his face sweating, hips moving. Were they making love? She felt so sick. She tried to bring her hands up to stop him but she was restrained.

Glass, shattering. Picture frames, window glass. She had screamed.

Oil on her forehead. Dean smeared it there with his thumb. Did he believe he was a priest? Not oil. Jelly. Conductive jelly. The kind they used on electrodes before . . .

. . . he hit the switch and her body jolted in a death dance.

This must be what the electric chair is like. I've never killed anyone.

Not yet.

"Get out," Dean said.

***

She woke at the end of the afternoon. The room was full of shadows. She lay weak in the arm chair he'd thrown her into, the sun long gone.

She huddled, weaker, in the corner, deep in the shadows.

"You had to push. You had to push and push and push. You couldn't just go along and let things be the way they needed to." Dean's voice is angry. Furious. He paces in front of her, scattering tepid sunlight that comes in through the living room windows. "You couldn't just let things happen. You couldn't *trust* me. I'm your doctor. I know what's good for you."

Laura trembled. The sun across her legs was distant, un-warm. She sat where Dean had dumped her in one of the easy chairs, too far gone to care what Dr. Dean "Amazing" Grace did. She held her hands up in front of her face and imagined she could see through them. Everything was small and lost, so far away it hardly seemed to matter. She was separated from herself, scattered as the motes of light Dean strode through as he paced. Here. Hands. Fingers splayed. There. Corner. Across the sunlight. With the others, dark shadows in a light room. Dual consciousness. She could hear herself thinking from the corner, the place where she crouched with the others.

Come back. Come back. Bring us just a piece, a strong piece of yourself.

Laura stared at her hand again. Cold sunlight fell across the nails. They looked like pearls. She crumpled the hand into a fist, tight, tighter, nails cutting into her flesh.

There was so much she'd never done. Never gone many places. Never met many new people.

In front of her, forward and back, Dean paced and raved.

Around her, all the shadows chittered and swirled. *What have you brought us? How strong are you? Can you pull us out? Can you send him away?*

Insistent voices. Dean, pacing, raving.

"Shut up." She stood, her fists curled. It felt good. Behind her the shadows dropped to whispers. In front of her, Dean stopped, amazed.

"What did you say?" Fury only a heartbeat away, still buried under shock.

"I said – SHUT UP." She swung her hands around together, fingers interlaced, caught him just under the jaw and sent him flying, his mouth open, his hands just rising. She sent him flying backward and he caught the back of his leg on something, his little black bag, maybe, and she saw him go down. Go down. Down. Slow motion fall. Until the sound. The crack, his head hit the wall behind him and he slid down it and lay very still.

Very still. Very, very still.

The shadows swarmed. Over the floor. Over Dean's body. They surrounded Laura, the shadows and the Laura part of the shadows, everything around her, everything surrounding her.

What else can you do? How can you help us? Can you set us free?

Her own voice just one of them.

She could, probably. But there were so many places she'd never been and so many people she'd never met and Laura – the other Laura – was kind of shy and stupid and if she stayed here, why, wouldn't they think she'd done it?

"Shut up," Laura said to the shadows and turned her back and walked out of the house and away from her life, starting over, somebody new.

"There are shadows in this house," the girl said and her voice held a note of unease. She stood in the living room, staring around at the bright spring sunlight, the overhead lighting and still the shadows that seemed to breathe. To pulse. As if they were alive.

"Turn a light on," he said. Big guy, grinning. He came up behind her from the kitchen, wrapped her in a bear hug and swept her off her feet into a circle. "Turn 'em ALL on. It's our house now!"

"It's our power bill, too," she said, grinning. They'd wanted their own house, waited and saved for it. And now . . . the grin slipped a little. Now there were shadows.

But he took her hand, tugging her upstairs to see the view from the bedroom window and where the bed would go and the wall they could knock out between rooms so the next room over could be where the *crib* would go, and she forgot the shadows in her delight.

Downstairs, the shadows slid and pulsed, and the Laura part of the shadows thought, *Come back. Help us. You were a part of me. How could you just leave?*

I wrote On the Cusp *for an anthology that was canceled before I even submitted the story. The collection was meant to be one of four, horror for every season. On the Cusp suggests that change can be very difficult.*

On the Cusp

Some time before noon she pulled the razor out of her bag and sat contemplating it. Such a simple thing, sharp and bright, clean and simple, creative and destructive. Sun glinted off the metal and made her eyes tear. The day was bright, almost painfully spring. She hated spring and always had. Her birthday was deep summer and spring was always like the beginning of a deadline for her – look how far through the year you are and still pasty white, no time to color up; still too fat, no time to slim down – and X amount of days before she was another year closer to death and farther from where she wanted to be. She was a perennial middle child, one of the ones who started things she couldn't finish, constantly made promises she couldn't keep. The unsettled one, volatile one minute, sunny the next, thin arms and fat through the middle. There were no extremes for her, or far too many.

The razor caught the sunlight. Pretty thing, all beautiful angles and sharp edges. She didn't mean anything by it particularly; it was just a reminder of the way things got for her when she wasn't paying attention.

"I'm paying attention," she said.

There were ducks nearby, the fat soapy kind, quacking at each other, waddling and fluffing. There were squirrels, there were lizards, there were small clean brightly dressed children heeding their mothers and playing quietly.

It was almost an absurd scenario. It was spring, and it had come late this year and summer was pushing up hard behind it, early and presumptuous.

She lifted the blade, put her lips against the flat side. When she inhaled she could smell warm metal but the blade was cool against her lips. She flicked her tongue out, tasted it. Soft. Smooth.

There was no one very close to her. Sun beat down where she sat on the bench surrounded by books and her knapsack and clothes.

Gently she drew the blade along the inside of her arm. The day was cool, the wind off the river brisk, but the sun was the perfect balance. "Just right," she whispered and turned the blade in her fingers. The sharp edge came down on her inner arm, left a slight white mark trailing behind it. She shivered and looked up. Everything was just as it had been. The children played, maybe a little louder. The mothers shushed, maybe a trifle more harshly. But the sun and the wind and the flowers and all – she sighed.

Beautiful day. She pressed harder with the cutting edge. The blade separated the top layers of flesh. Thin lines dotted with red trailed in its wake. One of the children screamed. She heard his mother say sharply, "Johnny, *shut up*." Another mother, concerned, reached out as if to comfort the boy and the first woman slapped her arm down. "Don't you think I know the right way to handle my son?"

Silence from the second woman, who looked hurt, and then, deliberately, shrugged, letting it go. She'd overstepped. That's all. No big. They went back to their conversation.

A parade of geese paused in the middle of the road and held a conversation that involved much unfolding of their raiment and much muttered cursing. Drivers sat and smiled but not as much as they had earlier. A couple checked their watches and frowned. Someone honked, short and sharp.

She placed the blade high on her inner forearm and dragged it down, applying pressure front and back. The blade slipped cleanly into her skin. The cut opened like a flower centered with darkness. She sighed and around her the day darkened. A wind came up. One of the children uttered a sharp cry of fury and another struck her with a toy. The girl's mother reached for her child's tormentor and began to smash her fists against his mouth while his mother howled and pulled at her, then turned her rage on the girl who turned without thinking and sank her teeth into the hands that flailed at her and threw her head back and howled at the darkened day.

Amy sat on the park bench and her blood dripped onto the grass. She was peaceful and violent and content.

It was partly cloudy or mostly sunny when Amy went in to work the next day. She wore long sleeves, which were too hot, but she had to anyway because of the fresh cuts on her arm. She settled at her desk, noticed that her trio of attorneys were marked out on the board, and decided she was on time after all. Someone had brought in an enormous bouquet of wild flowers – Costco, $7.99, she thought – and someone else had tacked up a poster of sun and surf (and sunburn, Amy thought) while someone else still sported snowmen on their desk.

I hate this time of year, Amy thought. The heat was on in the office – the usual musty gassy smell permeated everything in the old building, as if somehow they were on propane – and in protest someone else had turned on a fan. Amy sighed.

"Everything all right, Amy?"

Damn it. Lorna. So the office manager had seen her. No point trying to pretend she'd been on time now and no point in trying to argue that with all three of her attorneys missing in action it made no difference anyway. This was Lorna, and Lorna lived for messing up legal secretary's lives.

"You were a little late this morning. Just wanted to be certain everything was okay at home."

Amy gritted her teeth. *No you didn't.* Prying for the sake of prying vied in Lorna with prying for the pleasure of pointing out Amy was late and if she could inflict a little more damage by reminding Amy of some serious, home/life thing that had made her late, so much the better.

I will not glare, Amy determined and looked up and forgot all about Lorna's comments anyway.

Lorna wasn't alone. "I'd like you to meet Serena," Lorna said and the woman stepped forward.

She was everything Amy was not – tall and lush and full bodied. Her hair fell in waves of amber and gold and was obviously stunningly natural. Her body was the perfect expression of curves and straightaways. Full bodied, like a beer, and yet so perfect you just wanted to stare. She smiled, neat and tidy and confident, full of herself and when Amy rose to take her hand she knocked into her desk, bruised her thigh, caught herself on the plastic mat under her seat. She met Serena's eyes and thought, *She's my replacement*, and looked away.

Lorna hadn't stopped talking and Amy fell back into her stream of words. "Joining us and I know you'll be able to show her the ropes."

Amy felt a bright spear of panic. Secretaries were shown the ropes by Lorna and given overflow work from others and absorbed that way into the pool unless someone had quit.

Or unless someone was being replaced.

Amy worked directly for Misery, Axeman & Jokes, her private code for Mausert, Atcheson and Oakes. If she was showing Serena the ropes, she was showing Serena *her* ropes.

I'm training my own replacement.

When she surfaced from her thoughts, Lorna had departed; her last words still danced on the air, something about show her everything and Amy was alone with The Other Woman.

I need this job.

You're being paranoid. Maybe it's something else. Maybe someone is quitting or going on maternity. Maybe it's not you.

But she'd been late a lot this year and a couple times she'd blown up over something trivial and stupid and when she was good she was very, very good and Lorna admitted it. But all things change and good only lasted so long with Amy.

"Damn it."

Under her breath, but Serena still turned to her. Pink lips. Green eyes. "Excuse me?"

Amy shrugged. "Nothing. Sorry. I was late this morning and I'm still trying to get caught up."

Serena nodded. "We're all late sometimes." But her smile said otherwise. Serena wasn't late. Serena wasn't planning on being late. Serena was here, all sunshine and smiles and ready to go. Out with the old, in with the new. Full blown. In progress.

Amy started, and caught up again. "Let me show you around the office and give you a run down of the departments."

She didn't know what else to do.

By lunch Amy was disgusted. A dozen times during the morning she'd wanted to slip away to a quiet corner and find a blade and focus herself again. Just the raw intent of blood was enough sometimes when things were running out of control, and if something happened because of it, well, side effects happen. But Serena stuck to her like a thorn in a rampaging rose bush. When Amy finally looked at her watch and saw lunch was close enough to call it, relief made her light-headed. She was meeting Kath, stable, sensible, silly, fun Kath, who would laugh with her over Lorna's Lornaness and Serena's serene, untroubled perfection and add her own woes for good measure, her part time pay, full time responsibility job and her attention deficit husband and obsessive-compulsive offspring.

"So after lunch I'll show you the filing system," Amy started and even then she had her purse in her hands and her car keys and had begun to edge away when Serena said, "Oh, yes, I'd love to, thank you so much, it's always so difficult to find places to eat when you're new," and linked arms with Amy as if she were leading rather than following. Amy gaped and sputtered and the blade in her purse called dark magic to her but Lorna passed, beaming, approving, points in Amy's favor, and there was no good way out of it.

"–bathing suits in those rooms, the mirrors are like cameras, you know, they add weight to you and I think it sticks." Kath took a breath, took a bite of breadstick and waved it at Serena.

Who said, "Absolutely, they should be outlawed, they're the *worst*," and went back to her salad with no dressing and iced tea with no sugar and Serena had never worried for an instant about her weight, Amy would bet on it.

All lunch had been that way. Kath and Serena hit it off at once, like old home week, like a reunion of dear old friends and Kath told *Serena* her tales of woe and *Serena* told Kath *her* Lorna stories and even some of Amy's and Amy sat and fumed and excused herself once to the ladies' where she tried to bring on a small thunderstorm (they were, after all, eating outdoors) but when she got back to the table, fresh cuts neatly hidden under long sleeves, the sun was highlighting Serena's hair and Kath was basking in it and Amy just felt hot and sticky and ignored and angry. Even at lunch she couldn't shake the feeling she was training her own replacement.

"So I'll call you, right?" Serena said as Amy sat back down. Amy's eyes went wide and she tried not to stare when Kath said, "Of course, here's my number, this is going to be so much fun."

"What are we doing?" Amy asked brightly. *Brightly.* Excited. Included. Kath was *her* friend.

But both Serena and Kath suddenly sobered, lost their smiles and then put on polite ones and said, "Well, actually, Amy, it was just the two of us– "

Kath actually reached out and patted Amy's arm and Amy waited for the punch line but one didn't come.

"Oh." Tears in her throat. She put her napkin on her plate and fumbled with her purse. "I have to get back to the office – " because she couldn't say "out of here" but of course she'd brought Serena and she'd have to take her back and the three of them ended up on the street together, Kath and Serena talking as fast as they could to get everything said.

Traffic was horrendous, she was running late again and the car was across a major street, no signal nearby and she started across during a lull and made it to the median island, Kath and Serena behind her, still talking.

At least she'll be late too, Amy thought and the hand came out of nowhere, middle of her shoulder blades, and pushed full force. Amy spun into the street.

The van barreled down at her. Amy could see the driver's face, as terrified as her own, she had more chance of going forward than back but she was off balance. Her ankle twisted and she stumbled, caught herself, pushed off and felt the edge of the van brush her. The brakes screamed against asphalt as the driver swerved and braked and the back of the van swung hard behind her and knocked her flat but the van itself shielded her from cars behind it. Another car slammed into the van which rocked but held.

The world shook itself and Amy heard the driver, sharp exclamation and gears slamming into place and the struggle with the door. There were voices all around her, sharp and afraid and real time though everything else had slowed and she looked up to see Kath touch Serena solicitously – are you all right? – before she moved toward Amy, Serena following slowly, her expression unreadable.

Though it didn't look like concern.

Hot water bottle. Advil. Ice packs. Elastic bandages. Firm pillows. Remote control. Phone. Books. Water. Crutches. Kath made sure Amy had everything she needed, then fidgeted with her keys by the front door.

"Aren't you staying?" Amy asked. Trying to be charitable. Trying to sound like of course she expected her best friend to stay after the day she'd had. She'd been *run over*, after all. "We can order pizza. You could stay over." She stopped before she started to beg.

Kath twisted her key chain between her fingers. "Hon, that sounds– 'er, great. But we kind of– well, we were going– I've got plans." She looked hangdog. She looked ashamed. But she definitely looked like she was going.

"Oh. Well. Of course, if you have *plans*." She sounded bitter. She waved her hand and it was supposed to look flippant or cynical or light; it came off like Get Out.

Which was how she felt. Long damn afternoon – all the people and the ambulance and Serena and Kath hanging on to each other and staring down at her. The ER where they cut a perfectly nice pair of pants up the side only to discover that – like she'd said – her knees were naturally knobby like that. Serena drove them back to the office and Lorna said, "You're late, Amy" before she saw the crutches and the bruising and even then her attention seemed to be more on Serena who slipped behind Amy's desk and pulled up a file on her computer. One Amy had walked her through that morning.

My replacement, Amy thought, and managed to drive herself home. Any other time Lorna's assurances of, "Take your time, we just want you healthy" would have been welcome. This time it just sounded like, "We have someone else who can take your place. Go, already."

"I can stay if you really need me to," Kath said, drawing her back to the present.

Need. Not want.

She was losing everything. For a moment her heart pounded too hard for her to speak. Tears blinded her and she blinked furiously against them. As long as she kept them from spilling out both she and Kath could pretend. Kath had to want to stay. That was friendship. That was them. Amy's work had to want her to take her time and recover because she was valuable, not because they could afford her downtime with someone to cover for her.

Replace her.

Everything was spiraling out of control. No. Everything was slipping away, everything was becoming intangible, uncatchable. Everything was becoming someone else's.

She was being replaced, the old shoved out of the way for the new.

She needed to regain control. She had to put things back in order. Time was running out. Time was chaotic. She'd stop the chaos.

"No, I'll be fine," she told Kath. "Just hand me my purse before you go?"

Kath gave her a brief hug around the shoulders, as if Amy were incredibly fragile and old. Her purse dropped between them to the couch and Amy let it lay. "I've got my cell on, hon. If you need me, call." But again, not just because she wanted to. To talk. For company. For comfort. If you *need* me.

It's not every day you nearly die. It's not every day you nearly get killed, shoved into traffic. She'd felt the hand. Kath must have seen it. But Kath was going and the ache of abandoned was growing and side effects happen, don't they?

She let the purse lie, returned the hug, said yes and no and of course to things she couldn't have named even then, and finally Kath was gone and the golden spring evening leaned hard toward summer – almost here. Time's almost up. Spring was late this year (*you're always late*) and the season's almost upon us and *you're not ready*.

She dropped her head into her hands, rubbed her fingers hard over her face. She felt a million years old, over and used up. No one really needed her. Kath had moved on. Work had moved on. There were no recent boyfriends, no romantic ties and her family– memory felt brittle and thin. She rubbed her eyes until she saw bright spots of color, then looked up fast. Sound, like something scratched at the front door, but from the inside. Movement when she looked, too fast and fleeting for her to make it out but she saw *something*, wavering and uncertain and she called out before thinking about it, groped for her crutches without looking and got to her feet.

There was movement again, just beyond sight, and sounds coming from the kitchen. She hitched that way. No point in being quiet – anyone would hear her coming. She called out but got no answer. Maybe Kath had come back, in the back door into the kitchen, but when she got there she saw only movement at first, uncertain and unreal, just form and shape without substance. Amy leaned forward and strained, squinted into the sunlight, and saw Serena, moving about the kitchen as if forever familiar with it, making tea, cutting bright fruits and brilliant red tomatoes and Amy made an inarticulate sound, rage only, and threw one of the crutches.

It passed through Serena's form, clattered to the tile floor, and Amy knelt, breathing hard, watching future ghosts or past possibilities, tears on her cheeks already drying as if she were too far gone to exist, as if her pain was too unimportant.

Serena turned and smiled, the hard, sharp smile of the victor. Already she was more real, less possibility, more reality.

Amy turned with her remaining crutch, made her way back to the couch. Her heartbeat double timed – Serena would know where she was going and what she meant to do – but when she got to the couch she was alone again, the sounds had stopped.

She dropped to the cushions and dug through her purse.

The blade slipped neatly into the flesh of her inner arm. Always the way when she spun out of control, chaotic and confused, too many opposites at once – hot sun, cool breeze, love and hate, fat and slim, pasty white and out of time and Serena with Kath when Kath should have been with her, laughing about Serena.

The cold hard feeling of the inch-long blade between her fingers, the lines across her skin. The way the flesh peeled back because she was still young and her skin stretched tight. The blood hesitated and then flowed neatly into the channels and the world spun down to just this moment.

Amy sucked air, made a second cut and a third. Blood pooled and spilled over, ran across her arms and dripped. Peace started up in her. Calm. She reordered the world around her.

Blade transferred hands. She rarely ever cut with her other hand, her 'stupid hand' as Kath called it, and she missed Kath, didn't want to hurt her, but when Amy called order to chaos, sometimes things happened. Happened all the time.

"She made her bed," she whispered and cut the other arm, smooth, relatively unscarred. Carefully, because she didn't have control and wasn't used to it and the blade slipped in easily and neatly, calm straight lines, blood welling up. She took a breath. Another. If something happened, she was sorry. Happy, sad. Delighted, devastated. Partly cloudy, Kath called her; capricious.

The blade slid in again. Fingers slid out. Amy hesitated, only an instant. Jerked back in alarm, as if she could leave her own arm behind. An instant was all *she* needed. Fingers slipped from the cuts in Amy's arms, pushed up and out and flesh tore and shredded and between her shoulder blades and through her chest and in her hips she felt something pushing upward, levering up, pushing out, felt something inside her setting itself free, future out there, not in here.

Amy screamed, and the thing tore from her mouth. Blood splashed. The apartment around her rippled. Amy grabbed for the elastic bandages. It wasn't too late, she could pull the edges of the cuts together, seal the bleeding, close the exits, but even then Serena was pushing up and out and through, full blown, on time, summer to Amy's spring and she had time to think *My replacement* before she fell away.

I wrote The Forever Sleep after the events of both 9/11 and the American Airlines crash of November 2001, and Patrick Swenson gave it a wonderful home in both Talebones #26 and The Best of Talebones.
Sometimes reality just needs a reset. Fiction can give us that alternate ending.

The Forever Sleep

Not long after they'd given up on The Tonight Show and gone upstairs to bed, Jerry heard it coming. The drone of jet engines, too close, too low and something wrong. It was still some distance off but it was coming fast and he didn't figure he had a lot of time. Jerry's hearing was amazing – incredible – but a couple miles was nothing to a jet.

Christy was already gone, deep into a Forever Sleep. That's what she called it when she plunged over the abyss into sleep. Jerry hated the term but it was true – Christy asleep was Christy vacated. So Jerry alone was awake, the insomniac. The therapist kept suggesting biofeedback and self-hypnotism, said they were working for Jerry's daughter, and Jerry kept saying next week as if next week would have more time.

Speculation took maybe twenty seconds, maybe only ten, and then he was upright, half-dressed out of deference to a New York winter, Christy up and over his shoulder and the speed of sound coming towards them, increasing but not yet blotting out the world, the sound of the plane to the point where normally one looks up and wishes it would pass, maybe thumbs the remote to up the volume on the television. But it was there, increasing, coming closer, how many minutes away? Miles? Blocks? He had no time. He ran, Christy jolting against his back, downstairs to the pink bedroom where Carly lived, only she wasn't awake, their six-year-old insomniac, slipped off into her mother's Forever Sleep and she'd locked her door the way she'd been told time after time after time never to do.

The sound was on top of them, the plane a matter of blocks away. Seconds only. He figured he had three blocks, maybe less, and he could hear the wrongness in the engines, something, not the sound of a plane going overhead and *what did you say* and *wow, that's loud,* but the kind of misstep that sends planes down into the ground like gravity really does work.

He pounded on her door, shouted, solid wood under his fist and there was nothing on the other side, only silence, only sleep, and the plane filled the world– he'd lose them all. One last shouted "*Carly!*" before he ran.

Jerry ran, Christy coming awake, starting to surface, and vaguely combative, ran for the basement stairs, down them so fast one of them should have been hurt, into the sub-basement, old house, civil war days, revolutionary war days. There were tunnels. There were escape routes. Christy surfaced and screamed "Carly!" in a voice that sounded like jet fuel ignited and then the sound was on top of them and then there was.

Silence.

They held each other in the moments after, eyes wide and staring over each other's shoulders, starting into each other's eyes. Light flickered over them. Power held, somehow. A series of explosions shook the earth. The basement walls shuddered and held. Smoke filled their lair. They had to go further into the tunnels and up and out from there. Or back to the house.

"It's on fire," Christy said and was out of his arms before he could even grab for her.

"Please – " but he was following. Of course he was following, it was the only reason he wasn't leading. Wife and daughter, one he could get to and carry to safety, one he couldn't; how do you choose? Stairs like ice under his feet– he could feel them this time – and getting warmer as they went higher. When they pushed the door open into the house he expected flames. Instead the door from the basements opened into the engine, huge and filling the world. They blades had stopped spinning, stopped sparking, stopped doing whatever it was jet engines did. He turned to Christy to say, "I'm going in there," and she was already past him.

Convoluted. Like a nautilus shell. They doubled back on themselves time after time. There was nothing around them but the industrial gray of engine housing. They could move almost upright, trailing through as if finding their way through a maze. Farther in with every turn around curved metal fans blades, curved metal walls, they'd walked through the back of a blow dryer, or one of those industrial fans on buildings, but there was depth and there was trail and always they moved farther in and it was taking too much time, following Christy and when she fell, sobbing, Jerry pulled her up and took her hand and led the way.

Staging area next. Something. There was a place where engine ended and another world began. To their left and ahead they could see into the plane, frozen expressions on the passengers' faces. This was a lost place. A forever sleep. To the right and just ahead, where there should have been more plane and a way to the cockpit, no admission, crew only, there was instead a corridor of the same industrial airline gray. They didn't speak but followed. What would it be this time? Jerry thought. Terrorism, domestic or foreign. Human error. Another senseless tragedy. Why are planes routed over neighborhoods? Bad enough airports are ensconced in the heart of cities – and "Nothing's supposed to go wrong," Christy would say, those times he asked this aloud, and Jerry always said, "Well, of course it's not *supposed* to," and sometimes that ended the conversation and sometimes it didn't.

He moved faster. She was up ahead somewhere, his Carly – caught in the passages between life and death, safe for the moment in the Forever Sleep and they had to reach her before she woke.

"Are they dead?" Christy asked. They moved through the gray and around them the passengers sat in their seats, tray tables upright and seatbelts securely fastened, as if waiting for the seatbelt sign to go out so they could move freely around the cabin. Sat securely tucked in, neat and arranged, hands natural, faces rigid. "Jerry?"

"I think its their last minute," he said. "The last way they remembered looking before – " he spread his hands. Before the wreck they couldn't see, the crash that had shattered their homes and lives and somewhere up ahead Carly, please, god, in the Forever Sleep. "We have to get to her," Jerry said. Along the gray metal nowhere, curved walls either side and they were running into the stillness and silence, but the smoke and the sounds were starting to come in, starting to filter along the cracks in the metal (the cracks in the dream.) Hurry, he whispered, to Christy, to himself.

Running now, and their footfalls were hollow and he thought he could hear the very distant sound of sirens, likely the aircraft would have radioed for help and word would have gone out, it's going down and the location, pinpointed seconds after the crash but sirens already on the way and sirens always woke Carly, the insomniac six-year-old, even once she slept dreams couldn't hold her, she woke if people talked too loudly or a car went by trailing music or if a dog nearby barked a handful of times or if a siren went off in the city. Unless she fell into the Forever Sleep.

Long tunnel, gray, and webbed, he thought he could see through panels of it, understood, suddenly, the tunnels were concourses sent from terminal to plane, the carpeted accordion pleated covered walkways that stretched from Point A to Point B. They ran, their footfalls jolting the concourse, bouncing the fold-up walls, he could hear Christy's breath sobbing in and out, Carly's name under her breath but not loud enough to wake her, please let her be in a Forever Sleep, one of the times Carly toppled over and down into sleep as deep as her mother's. Please let her be dreaming. Let her be waiting.

"It's changing," Christy said. She slowed. Jerry wanted to keep running. "Jerry, listen."

He followed her example, slowing, his footsteps quieter until they stood together, listening. Dull gray corridor and there had been sound minutes ago, something past the panicked pounding of their feet, the bouncing of the moveable throughway. A sound like the engine, Jerry thought now. Like something mechanical, failing. Like the plane had sounded as it headed for their home.

"Jerry?"

He put his hand up against her. "Wait." Soft sound. Vibrating. Like something gearing up. Idling. Like a plane on power but not ready to taxi. "Something's changed it," he said and Christy looked like she was going to say something, instead turned and ran, further along the corridor, in the lead again, and Jerry followed.

The plane formed around them, plane as it might look to someone who ad only flown a couple times. Outline, only. Seats, aisles, overhead compartments, windows. The aisles were wrong, though, the seats something like school desks. The doors to the plane had changed. Everything askew.

"What is it?" Christy asked.

"She's changing it," Jerry said. The aisle stretched out in front of them, impossibly long. Passengers lined up in the seats, facing straight ahead, eyes open, chests moving but otherwise as stick figured as the passengers they'd passed at first.

"Carly," Christy breathed and Jerry whispered, "Shhh," moved forward, gray becoming color, color becoming pink and Christy's intake of breath behind him, when he turned she had covered her mouth with one hand. The other hand reached for his. Jerry took it tightly and turned the doorknob to his daughter's room.

The unlocked door opened easily.

Pink, the way she wanted it. Princess pink, Disney pink, six-year-old girl pink and in the center of it Carly slept in a tangle of limbs, mouth slightly open and eyes squinched shut in the Forever Sleep.

The room filled with the sound of the jet engine the way Jerry had never heard it– strong, steady. There was no tremor, no uncertainty, no underlying sound that signaled something was wrong. Just the jet, the way Carly had heard it, before Jerry did, far enough out that nothing had gone wrong yet, Carly the insomniac whose hearing put Jerry's to shame, who heard the first foreign note enter the plane's refrain. And then? And then forced herself to sleep, the therapist's biofeedback or relaxation training or whatever technique she used working for her as it had yet to work for Jerry. Carly the insomniac with enough time to throw herself into one of Christy's Forever Sleeps, enough time to enter into the land of dream. In Carly's world the plane continued overhead, the engines strong and steady. In Carly's world, her family was safe.

"Carly," Christy said and Jerry jolted. The sirens were closer still.

"Don't." He said it so quietly she didn't hear him and started to speak again. Jerry moved faster, hands up over her mouth, his movement shocking her, her daughter's name cut off. "She's holding it off," he said and Christy stared at him, hands gesturing.

"You can't mean – we can't let her sleep – " she fumbled over the last word, "forever."

There were tears on his cheeks, cold in the night air. The sound of sirens was closer. Christy would hear them soon. Carly would wake. He heard the sirens and smelled acrid smoke, oily, dark and chemical. It had already happened and not yet, a fact held in abeyance. The world breathed between possibilities. Christy looked from husband to daughter, mouth opening. Smoke billowed. Sirens crept closer. Carly whimpered and moved restlessly. Jerry panicked, one look at Christy, begging her not to speak, and then he scooped up Carly, flushed face close to his, held her the way he did when she'd fallen asleep during a car trip and he carried her in to her bed. Carly mumbled and let her head fall against his chest. Jerry wasted an eternal instant staring down at her before he motioned to Christy, *come on*, back toward the tunnels. Christy first, ducking slightly as she entered the metal corridor, as though the ceiling of the walkway had lowered slightly, hemming them in. Jerry frowned at it even as he followed her in, waited just for an instant to see what the plane was doing. Hum of jet engines, strong and steady and then, for an instant, for a heart stopping moment, the engine stuttered.

Carly was waking, shuddering in his arms as she tried to hold on to sleep.

Jerry ran.

Christy was in front of him. Her footsteps sent back panicky shuddering echoes. The walls were closer now, the ceiling lower. Their concourse was shrinking, the way back closing.

"Sleep," he whispered, running, trying to move gently, arms tight and straining as he tried not to bounce his daughter. "Sleep and re-dream it." Change it. Faces of the passengers filled his mind, the people they'd passed on the way in, real as if Carly hadn't simply peopled them, real as if they somehow ran here, real and not dreamed. "Sleep, baby. Daddy's here."

The engine loomed, maze of metal leading back to their home, and the blades were beginning to turn, whir of motion behind him with every turn he made, the jet engine coming back to life. Carly coughed. Her eyelids fluttered.

"Sleep," again, they were supposed to be investigating self hypnosis, a single word that could lead either of them to the brink of sleep, but they hadn't started yet, next week he kept saying to the therapist, so much else going on in life. What would Carly's word be? Pink? Safe? Sleep? "Sleep."

The basement door loomed. Christy hit it, fumbled at the latch, fell through the opening in front of them. Behind them the jet engine tore into life, churning air, blades spinning. The sound of the plane filled the night, closer than when Jerry had first heard it and everything wrong throbbed in it, the sound of mechanical systems failing. Failed. The plane was screaming towards them. Christy stumbled on the stairs. Jerry caught her, jolted Carly.

"Daddy?"

"It's all right, sweetheart."

"I love you. Mom, love you. It's all right."

Plane on top of them, sound filling the world, down the carved earth stairs, sub-basement, everything was not all right.

"I'm all right," Carly said and Christy stopped running as if she'd hit an invisible wall, jolted back against them, "Carly, no!" But the six year old insomniac smiled, older than her years, somehow, loving and sad and said, "It already happened. And it's all right," before she looked at each of them one more time and slipped and slid away into the Forever Sleep.

Christy and Jerry stood, arms around each other, around their daughter, and overhead the sound of the engines changed, one last time, mechanical equipment catching, impossible sound of acceleration and lift, engines screaming as the jet climbed, passed, away from the house, away from the city, gravity defied once again and the plane climbed. Inside, the pilots, no doubt sweat soaked and chilled, radioed the tower– we're all right, we're coming down normal, keep emergency on hand– inside, no doubt, passengers held their breath, hands clasped together, strangers holding strangers, cabin sharp with the chemical smell of adrenaline and terror.

The plane passed overhead and Jerry held Carly, insomniac no longer, Christy smoothed her daughter's soft hair and rained kisses and tears on her cheeks as forever Carly slept.

Sometimes stories happen when disparate elements come together. In this case it was fear of the other combining to become both the at-risk teens in lock-down facilities – and vampires. At the time I wrote it I was working through local arts programs in various juvenile justice and rehab facilities. The moment of connection with Anthony actually happened – as for the vampires…?

Thirteen

Me and my friends. Drive at night. Fast. Drive drive drive. Drinkin' and driving and there's a 'fro in the road not one of ours 13. Keep going. Drive. Night time's the best. Nobody owns me. Me and my crew. Ese. Shock cars. Cholo vans. Hip hop drive and wind at night in the summer full of dirt feels like needles against my skin, needles kissing. Kiss kiss. Drink deep. Bang on the door. 22 the window. Wake the white folks. Drive.

She knows what she's supposed to say. No, Anthony. No no no. You cannot write about drugs or gang banging or use 13 or refer to your Hispanic nature or say 'fro or talk about needles. She's the adult, the artist in residence with a group of at-risk kids in a facility. No, Anthony, no no no.

Never mind he prefers Tony. Never mind it's his name. He's *here*, he's trapped, he's subject to the Great American Social Services Continuum of Help. Help until you gag on it, one nation under *Us*, the ones who set the stage and make the rules and You. Do not. Fit in.

She knows what she's going to say.

"I really like your description of the dirt in the wind. I've felt that at night here. It feels like summer."

Tony just glares. Sullen. Fifteen going on god-knows how old. His eyes turn from vulnerable to violent with a response time any German engineer would kill for and she absolutely believes both.

Tony's keepers only believe the violence.

"You're not supposed to write about – "

"Yeah, whatever. But they always say write about what you know."

She forces her eyebrows to stay down. So he was listening at some point to someone. And he could write. If he wanted to. But she's not fooled.

A week ago they made contact. A connection. Sudden, startling. Short. Tony mentioned a movie– a drama, a new one, something he'd liked– and Jess hadn't seen it. Or anything else currently in theaters they'd all been discussing. Tony asked if she liked movies and she said she did, just as an artist with a carpenter husband they didn't have a lot of money and didn't see a lot of movies.

And Tony, sanely, rationally, without anger, said with his dad run off and his uncle in jail and him here, he was real worried about his mom and his little sisters. He understood not having enough money and he wanted to help them and he hoped things got better for her. Jess.

As if to make up for the lapse his next writing exercise – which he insisted on reading to everyone present, including staff – was about gang banging and going out at night to shake up the old white people and to terr-or-ize, breaking rearview mirrors along the street.

It was, irritatingly enough, well written, but the middle aged staff matron – mushroom white, brittle, humorless, who 'oversaw' the class but refused to join in – didn't see any artistic merit and Tony earned himself lockdown just like any real jail, just like the jail his uncle was in.

It wasn't a real jail, McGee Center. Jess wasn't even sure of its official designation – McGee Center for Troubled Teens? McGee House of Horrors? McGee Center for the Performing Arts? It was a dumping ground, for those who Didn't Fit Into the System.

It housed Frankie, fifteen, lesbian, unwanted by her mother, raped by her step-father, and looking curiously like Val Kilmer.

And Diana, who clutched a bible at all times and insisted her father was a preacher, that she was a gang banger (white blond, blue eyed, somewhat more than pleasingly plump), that she'd done hard drugs. She looked like the only thing she could be found guilty of was overeating.

There were two Hispanic girls, who along with Frankie were the Fa's – they appended 'fa' to the end of their names for no very good reason and acted obnoxious whenever allowed to sit together.

There was the mandatory Kid Who Could Not Shut Up, who incarnated into every class Jess ever taught, the sexpot who wore more eyeliner than three people generally did and the ubiquitous round kid who stuttered or smelled bad or scratched and who was generally on the edge of a psychotic break.

There were also two of the type of girls who seemed to cycle through every juvenile system, turning up at every facility Jess taught at and therefore taking her class at least three times every year. Each time they'd claim to love it though they rarely wrote anything coherent or longer than two lines. One of them raised her hand now and wanted to read what she'd written. Their topic had been "Night." Jess smiled, nodded, waited while the girl tried to decipher her own handwriting and started.

"They're here again," she read, solemn as any beat poet on open mic night. "Dozens of them, all around me. The music is so loud tonight. The mix master is playing everything I love and the loud and the hot mix until I dance and I pretend they're not there but they are. All the time. People say there's no such – "

"Stop reading this *instant.*"

Jess cringed. They had a code worked out. Anyone who saw Mrs. Thayer come in was supposed to start tapping a pen on the table. No one was tapping. Tony, however, was smirking.

Fine. He'd been in lockdown because of something he'd written. Getting Jess in trouble would make them even?

Jess sighed. Stood. "Janet." She'd specifically learned Thayer's first name, putting them on even footing.

"You know they can't talk about such things."

"You know I've asked you not to interrupt my class."

If bland, jowly looks could kill. Or even cause bruising. "I will *not* be spoken to–"

"Me neither," Jess said. "Let's go in the hall. Guys, your topic is 'The last time I' and I can hear you from the hall. Write. Write. Write."

The hall was quieter than the multi purpose room. Janet Thayer seemed to absorb all ambient noise. Even the florescent lights stopped humming. Jess thought about challenging her, waiting to see which of them broke and spoke first.

She disliked the woman's company too much to wait it out.

It was all the same thing anyway, Thayer pushing her weight around. The kids were not allowed to use any profanity, write about drugs, gangs or violence. In other words, everything they knew.

Jess wanted them to *write*, not think, not censor, not be afraid, but write. Create. Do. And so she pushed fiction at them. Use imagination. Not a gang banger. A – vampire.

No, said administration. No no no. Because that had just started, about the time Jess had said that. Night clubs, back doors, old rusted out cars. People were appearing there, dazed and frightened, with splitting headaches, traces of date rape drugs in their systems, bite marks on their necks.

Vampires were the newest thing. Suddenly bouncers and cops were pulling pronged (fanged!) necklaces off people's necks, which led to hard rubber substitutes which led to hard rubber substitutes with needles in them which led to more holes in people's necks and more arrests. Cottage industries sprang up. Mouth pieces with fangs that acted as filters. On the spot HIV tests. *Don't bite if it's not rite!* Jess was more appalled at the purposeful misspelling than the message. Couldn't you be an idiot and still spell?

Now vampires were spreading from the nightclubs and deaths were following. The whole scene appealed to the kids. Let them write about it. They wrote things out of their systems. They worried at her. Confided. Gossiped. Were catty. They wrote horror fiction that was thinly disguised fact and sometimes, briefly, it made a difference.

No, said Administration. No no no. N'no vamp– va– vamp-vamp-vampires. They said it enough it sounded like hip hop the vampires played. Death hop. Imagine heavy metal played to hip hop.

That was evil.

Vampires were myth.

Janet Thayer, unfortunately, was not.

Jess took a deep breath and attacked first.

"Did you get in trouble?"

"Of course not!" (*Yes.*)

"Are you going to stay?"

"Of course so!" (*I hope so.*)

"Damn!"

But Frankie was grinning.

"Yeah, yeah, you know you love me. Okay, who wrote?"

Oh, everybody. Such a responsible group. Everybody wrote, nobody talked and no idea why the storage pantry door was open or a pen lodged in the acoustical ceiling tile and it was time to go, those who were day-timers had buses to catch and those who always wanted her to drive them somewhere were begging rides. She offered to keep their writing for them, and Frankie had to tell her something, and Diana wanted to read her something, so she almost missed Tony slipping her his work to keep. He never did that, mostly tossed it or slouched away with it, and she met his eyes – no comfort there, hard cold mean, older than he should be – but took the papers and extricated herself and drove home in the sudden silence the end of class always left her in.

Barry had the news on when she walked in, turned up as if he was deaf as a post. She'd just missed another report on vampires.

"A real report?" she asked skeptically.

"No, another batch of mismatched facts, speculation and interviews with the mildly mad."

Jess nodded distractedly and dumped the McGee papers, searching for the mail.

"The murders are something though," Barry said. "They're just kids doing this vampire stuff. Do you think your kids could kill?"

Jess paused, thinking of Tony, thinking of the tattooed '13' on his arm, and slowly nodded.

Barry's self-satisfied snoring drove Jess out of bed. For her, insomnia was rare, but total. But once in her office, the urge to work, read or write, vanished.

"Then why are you awake?" she asked herself logically.

"Oh, let's see. Money. Work. Assignments I've got. Assignments I want. Fear of no more assignments when these are finished." She spun her chair back to face her desk. "The kids at McGee."

She stared at the blank screen.

"Janet Thayer."

Ahh. There it was. She'd talked to the executive director at McGee but no help there – they wanted someone in the room with her when she taught, for her own protection of course, certainly not just to make sure nobody even dreamed of writing on forbidden subjects. Certainly not to stifle any of the fun and creativity.

They try to suck all the fun out of everything, Jess thought. Her eyes felt heavy, as if identifying what was keeping her awake had gone some distance to fixing it. *Like the kids are all in jail after all. It's not rehab, it's storage.* Just last week one of the two Anna's had actually dared to ask a question while Jess explained something and Thayer had promptly snapped at her not to interrupt. Anna subsided instantly, never asked her question, and wrote nothing very much the rest of class.

Jess sighed. She'd tried to talk to Thayer about it but the woman treated *her* like an at-risk teen (20 years past it, thanks, Jess thought) and told her in no uncertain terms that the kids <u>had</u> to learn respect.

Jess bit down on every response that came to mind. If she wanted to stay at McGee, she had to contend with Janet Thayer. And if Janet Thayer wasn't playing the role of Janet Thayer, somebody else might, and might even be worse.

Go figure.

She needed to stay. The kids needed an outlet and a couple times a year she'd find somebody with real talent to encourage. They liked her classes. They gave her their work to read when they didn't want to read it aloud. They were locked up, bored and scared.

Scared. They were, actually.

Her eyes opened again and Jess frowned. Four month residency and the references to vampires had started during the first week. Now they were nearly constant. It wasn't just the media barrage and fascination – it was something else.

It was the Annas' longing.

It was Diana's bible.

It was Tony's fear.

Jess jolted, and stood abruptly. She'd dropped everything by the front door when she got home. Avoiding the squeaky board in the hall she collected it all and thumbed impatiently through three months of bad handwriting and grubby pages. Impossible not to find them – he'd handed them to her today – and then she had Tony's spiky pages in her hands and her heart thudded uncertainly and she didn't know why.

Poems. Or poem-shaped lines. Jess stared, nonplused. Tony's writing. That she recognized. A sheaf of papers, and she fanned them too fast, looking for an explanation, then slowed down to make another pass.

The pages on top were song lyrics. Hip hop. Rap. Something. They weren't even disguised except to the casual glance. He hadn't written these. They were cover. And on the bottom, a page about gang-banging and guns, something so completely what he wasn't supposed to be writing about it was a rather obvious distraction.

She pulled out the page sandwiched between them.

They're everywhere. Can you help? They know when you know. It's not a game. It's not just on TV. 'Lissa and Marie and Mama are alone and 'Lissa's getting interested. Too interested. She's clubbin. I can't help in here. Thayer watches me like I'm an animal. Night jerkoff's do bed count. She's my baby sister. I've got the tat but nobody gonna help until it's true. I lied. It's not 13 yet. My boyz – I talk big. I'm a boy. They won't help until I 13. They won't protect my family.

All hard and fast, and written as if he had to get the words on paper before his courage gave out. This was the Tony she'd met for less than a minute, the Tony that let his guard down and talked to her human to human.

Jess swallowed. *They're everywhere. It's not just on TV.* Tony was afraid. His spiky handwriting had grown more tight and sharp, as if he'd written faster and faster toward the end.

She turned the page over. On the back he'd written simply *Please help.*

Jess dropped the pages on her keyboard, dropped her head into her hands and sat staring at the weave of light between her fingers.

He needed her to get him out. How? She had one 90 minute class a week and no contact with the kids outside of it. She'd need to wait a week before she could even talk to him and then Thayer would be there.

Her shoulders slumped, jaw settled onto the heels of her hands. She closed her eyes.

There's no such thing as vampires. It's all media bullshit. It's all hype and razzle dazzle and marketing and fake teeth and teenagers.

"This is ridiculous," she said aloud and a hand came down on her shoulder, a voice close to her ear said something. Jess screamed.

"I didn't mean to scare you," Barry said.

"Then why did you sneak up on me?" Her heart hammered.

"It's the middle of night, you're not in bed, I called your name twice and got no answer." He looked reasonable. "Plus with that board in the hall nobody is going to sneak up on anybody. Maybe this weekend I ought to– "

" – take a look at it?" Jess grinned. He'd been saying that for two years.

Barry smirked. "Yeah. That. Why are you up?"

Suddenly, she didn't want to share. She was too sure of her sudden knowledge, too aware of how fast it could turn to disbelief again. Tony needed help. Tony was scared. And she didn't know what he'd done to land in McGee but she was relatively sure he wasn't a good kid badly misjudged.

It didn't matter. It didn't even matter that she'd guessed what 13 meant, or that Tony had lied about it and planned to change it. What mattered was right now she believed. Vampires or not, Tony's fear for his sister was real.

She wasn't quite ready to tell Barry she was planning to spring one of her kids because she believed he was a vampire hunter, that his family was in danger and that the 13 tattooed on his arm was soon going to be reality, not prophecy. Thirteen murders. Thirteen deaths.

Thirteen vampires.

Barry went back to bed. Jess went back to her computer to outline her options.

Problem: getting Tony out of McGee so he could help his family.

Problem: help defend his family against vampires didn't sound like anything the court system would understand.

Problem: help defend his family against vampires didn't sound like something she'd still believe in the morning.

Jess stared at her outline so far. Great, she'd defined the problem. There was also the How To part: how to defend her actions if she got caught. How to explain to Barry she'd apparently lost her mind.

Dandy.

She closed her eyes and started typing, something, anything. Insane ideas. Tony had a better chance of growing wings and flying out of McGee than getting out through any of these wild ideas.

Something moved. Something made a sound. Jess' eyes flashed open. Barry up again, looking for her? Only minutes had passed, surely. She hadn't slept, hadn't lost time in a writing frenzy.

Movement from the corner of her eye and she snapped her head around, saw something beyond her window other than the overgrown rose bushes. Heard something from beyond the hall.

The trembling started in her pecs, spread until she shook everywhere. She heard the screen door's characteristic squeal and no way had Barry gone out, he'd gone back to the bedroom; she'd heard him.

The screen banged against the railing. She had a second to think *It's just the wind* before she heard claws against the door again and something thudded. She got to her feet, went into the hall and couldn't go any further. Her heartbeat so fast she felt breathless. Her hands against each other cold and wet. Nothing could make her step into the living room where neither of them ever remembered to draw the curtains at night.

The sound came again. Claws. Thump. The doorknob rattled. Jess thought about Barry, asleep in the bedroom, and about Tony, locked away, unable to help his family. She thought about what he'd written. "They know when you know."

"Shit," Jess said, and stepped into the living room.

Cold. Dead. Haunted. Angry. White flesh, greenwhite of corruption, cadaverous white, flesh striped like shattered silk, runnels of flesh over the skull, eyes so black they were the night around them, empty sockets and empty eyes but they moved, tracking her, sentient, angry, wrong. This was no beautiful teenager outside a club, no joke, no game, no media darling. *They know when you know.* Locked in place, she stared, not breathing, not moving.

The thing turned and grinned at her through the window. The tongue lapped out, long, unnatural, bright red, across the lips. The thing smiled its contentment at her.

Jess felt the floor rush up under her. Her flailing hands grabbed and the floor lamp came down at her, struck her shoulder and hit the wall. Jess blinked as her teeth came together hard and when her eyes opened, it was gone.

"You had a nightmare," Barry said again and Jess let her breath out in a sharp hiss.

"How could I have a nightmare when I wasn't asleep?"

Barry spread his hands. "Love, nothing else makes any sense. You were tired, you were writing. You had the kids on your mind and that crazy note from Tony and the report on the news. You fell asleep, that's all– it was a dream."

"I was in my *office*. You're saying I dreamed myself into the living room?" He'd picked her up from under the floor lamp, hadn't he?

"Sleep walking," Barry said and she snorted.

"Right. I just happened to pick tonight to start." But he wasn't going to listen. He started the next sentence with, "Look, Jess, I know that you think – " and that was always the end.

He held out his hand and she took it and after he fell asleep again she lay awake trying to figure out how to get Tony out of McGee and somewhere deep in the night she looked past the not-quite-closed curtains and saw a pale and terrible face of shredded flesh and hunger and hatred but it couldn't get in and she closed her eyes and counted and when she looked again it was gone. And just before dawn she looked into the corner of the room where streetlight shined in and saw a pale and luminous being of beauty and elegance but that was a human, a child of beauty and media and that was the dream and so she slept.

In the morning she felt as if she hadn't slept at all.

Summer and hot. She dressed and wandered into her office and stared at the plans on the monitor – call McGee and claim to be Tony's sister

Family emergency. But she didn't know Tony's last name. Minors, and all that.

Or call in a bomb threat and see if they herded everyone outside. Without staff. Right.

Call McGee, tell them she left something there and needed to come get it. But what – keys? Wallet? Sanity?

Call McGee, tell them vampires were out to get her and she needed Tony's help.

Oh, why not?

She made coffee, showered, dressed again, reviewed everything she was supposed to do today, glanced at the living room window where the face had been and froze. Panicked. She had to do something, had to tell Barry. Had to spring Tony.

"It wasn't a nightmare," Jess said and went and got her keys.

The facility was on the edge of the city to the east, surrounded by University experimental farms, redolent with cut hay and cows. A handful f buildings shared parking lot space. Lots of windows in the buildings.

Jess scrunched down in her seat and pretended she was invisible.

Just before noon McGee opened up and disgorged teenagers across the lawn. Kids everywhere and only three staff from the looks of it. Jess sat up and watched.

Now what?

"Can I help you?"

The initial jolt rocked all her bones together. Her teeth snapped shut. *Damn.*

"I was here teaching a writing class yesterday and today I can't find my driver's license anywhere. I'm retracing my steps."

The staffer – somebody Jess had only seen from a distance in administration – nodded and frowned. "Why didn't you come in?"

Jess gulped. Patted her purse. "Phone call."

"Well, come on. We'll check."

They crossed the grass and Jess tried to catch Tony's eye but he just glared at her, sullen. *You big screaming idiot,* Jess thought and followed staff for a pointless search.

Next brilliant idea?

She pulled out of McGee's parking lot and headed back toward home. *Now what? If he's what I think he is, I need him as much as his family does.*

She glanced into the rearview, saw a face and drove into the curb and killed the motor.

"Smooth," Tony said.

"Fuck you," Jess said. "You scared me to death."

"Language!" Tony said in a good approximation of staff speech.

"Oh, your virgin ears."

"My virgin nothing, chica. Are you going to help me?"

Jess gestured. "Hello? Did I just get you out of there?"

He clambered into the front seat beside her and started giving directions. Jess laced her hands on the steering wheel without restarting the car.

"What are you waiting for? Mi familia–"

"It's just after noon," Jess said. "And I need your help too." She looked at him and didn't say anything else and Tony looked from the window at her. He could run now. He could do anything. Kill her. Take her car. His eyes were mean as the creature she'd seen at the window last night. She wouldn't look away. "How did you put it? 'They know when you know'." She stared and slowly his eyes changed.

"I can teach you," he said finally. "It's not that hard."

Nightmare. Some of them were kids, teens dressed in purples and blacks with rusty streaks of red in their clothing. Fang necklaces and glittered skin, they danced with abandon and suckled each other's throats in dark corners.

The rest were unmistakable, shorn of humanity. Their eyes lit with unholy hunger, their fingers curled toward the living. Saliva clotted crepe skin. They stank and lusted and killed. Anyone who could mistake one for the other was insane.

She stood at the edge of the crowd, waiting to go inside. Tony stood beside her. In between the vampires, old and new, real and play, there were the hopeful, the ones who longed, the indifferent, the indulgent and the indeterminate. There was Barry, at home, who maybe never would have seen the face at the window.

"How?" She gestured, and looked at him, and Tony understood and nodded.

"Not everyone sees them." He pointed to the news cameras, after the Real Story and Missing the Point. "They don't get it. It doesn't fit in two minutes before the weather." He pointed at a knot of black and purple play vampires. "They don't see it because it wouldn't be cool. 'Lissa doesn't see it because it would just be her big brother telling her what to do."

Jess shook her head. "Then why do we see it?"

Tony shrugged. "You lie." Before she could argue, "You said that about stories once. They're lies. So maybe you can see lies."

He stopped and Jess looked at him. "And you?"

Tony shrugged. "Come on."

She saw the others just before the entered the club. Nightmare time again. They looked like Tony, not because they were young, Hispanic and male, but because they shared a purpose, their faces stony and mean and Jess shivered in the impossibly hot club, grateful she'd come in with Tony. Half a dozen, maybe more, two shirts each, t-shirt under tailored. Baggy jeans. Tattoos. She swallowed and saw Tony point at her, saw the others nod, and then saw rapid fire hand signals as the gang spread out around the perimeter of the club, creating a net to trap the unwary. Slowly they drove the dancers together, tightening the knot at the center of the dance floor until someone screamed, sudden and jarring above the ear-splitting decibels of hip hp and rage. Someone screamed, and there was blood.

It fountained up above the crowd, geysered and splattered down like red sprinkler. People flailed at each other, everyone human desperate to get off the dance floor, every vampire grabbing, mouths twisted, cheated of their willing sacrifices. Claws reached, fangs clashed, one vampire tore into the neck of a screaming blond girl, bit through flesh and bone and a spray of crimson. His tongue worked greedily and he snapped at other vampires who got too close.

The gangbangers spread out, moving through the crowd. They carried stakes and knives and they dispatched without compunction. The floor turned crimson, sticky, wet. Jess gagged, the stench of rotted meat, metallic blood, perfume and alcohol, stepped back and slipped. Her heel caught on something, another person, the edge of the dance floor, something, and she started to fall. Hands caught her. Before she could turn, claws dug into her biceps and something shook her hard, tried to force her head to one side. Jess thrashed, kicked back, forced herself forward, felt freefall as the hands gave way. Behind her the creature fell, staked from behind and someone in a checkered shirt handed her a knife and shoved her back into the melee.

"Wait!" But her voice was lost in the storm inside the club and this was what she'd come to learn. They know when you know.

Bile in her throat again. She just wanted to fight free of the crowd. Jess waded forward and another rose up in front of her, yellowed teeth, ancient eyes.   It   reached   for   her   and   Jess   struck   first.

The stake sank like a knife into a rotting vegetable. She felt nausea rise even as the thing fell away and another rose up. The club broke with panic; suddenly everyone inside saw vampires and everyone – even the glitter vampires – wanted *out*. The first wave of panicked teens hit her and Jess went down hard, lost under flailing limbs, suddenly sure she'd be killed in the exodus, trampled past anything that could interest a vampire.

A hand reached down, pulled her free. She never saw who it was; by the time she turned the person was gone.

She turned back to the dance floor in time to deflect fangs heading right at her, had enough time to determine it was a kid, someone confused enough to still be playacting at this point. She shoved him hard in the direction of an exit, turned to see a vampire sink its teeth into a young girl's neck, and plunged her stake into its back.

Time stretched out, and the dance continued.

Past midnight. The artist in residence and the gangbanger sat on the curb and watched the cherry/blueberry lights strobe the club half a block away.

Jess' gaze was distant. She'd called Barry at some point, just to let him know she was all right. After he started yelling she hung up and gave the phone back to Tony. She didn't think it was his but didn't see the point of asking. Instead she asked, "Will you be able to help your sister?"

He grinned like a kid but the transition no longer rattled her. "'Lissa was there. She got out but before, I made her *see*."

Jess nodded. It made sense. Just like it made sense that she herself could see. Maybe Tony was right. Maybe it was because she was a writer. Maybe because Tony had the ability to let people see. Either way, she thought she and Barry were safer now. Tony's family, too. And she was starting to think Tony was better off out than in when it came to McGee.

McGee. Thayer. Cadaverous, dried out, emaciated and joyless. She'd find some way to hold Jess responsible for Tony's disappearance. Without ever knowing it was true. She pictured Thayer again and a thought struck her. Eyes still closed, sleep threatening despite where she sat, she asked thickly, "Do you think Thayer is a vampire too?"

She'd never heard Tony laugh before. He actually had a very pleasant laugh. "No," he said finally. "Thayer is just a bitch."

Jess nodded and watched the commotion at the club a bit longer and finally she said, "What are you going to do now?"

"Hang with my boyz. Keep a low profile. Stay out of McGee. Keep

'Lissa in line. Get a job."

She smiled. "We'll miss you in writing group."

He just smirked and she laughed. She stood to leave and pointed down at his arm. "And thirteen?"

"Thirteen," Tony said. "True." He raised his brows at her.

"One," she said. "No, two."

"You'll get there."

It struck her as funny. "I'm done. Out. Gone. Finished."

"*Pero*, no. Sorry. You never forget how to see."

I've always wanted to open an unmarked door somewhere in a city and step into another world, or step sideways and find myself in unmarked territory, somewhere off the map.
...or maybe not.

Thursdays in the Rain

On Thursdays the day-old bread store had a sale: buy one, get one, and it wasn't just bread, either; they had pies and pastries and sometimes even cookies. The four of them liked to walk down there early, pick up whatever they had the money for, and walk back home. The streets would be empty at that hour, pre-business rush, and while they walked they'd look into the storefront windows of cafes and restaurants and make the pin-striped clientele nervous. Angela had dreds, her once who-knows-what-color hair bleached and tinted and cellophaned and sprayed into bright orange and purple coils. Her piercings and Trent's tattoos were fairly fierce. Matt slouched along in oversized boots and a greatcoat, his hair bleached teddy bear color, and his mind somewhere far away. And of course Tory was tall, too tall, taller than women were supposed to be, six-three probably, and that alone was enough to make brief-cased cell-phoned businessmen nervous.

They never knew who was going to be at the store, tiny withered Louise with her steel-gray hair and her housedresses and her quick wit. Louise always stuffed extra goodies into their bags without charging them. Her daughter Lucy – hardened, sun wrinkled with square, mannish hands – glared through sullen eyes and rang them up and you could hear her cataloging them as she went: ugly, street trash, queer, lesbian. She didn't bother with their stories because she already knew. The four of them took turns on the way home, part of the ritual when Lucy was in the store, took turns making up stories to suit her. She was a recent divorcee who had lost her humanity in the settlement. She was a robot – no, a Vulcan – well, something emotionless and inhuman. She was an artist who had lost her muse.

"No," Angela said. "She used to have rages. But she came so close to killing someone during one she's on court-ordered lithium now to control them."

The others stopped talking and waited for Angela to go on. "What?" she asked and then they were all talking at once. "I made it up," Angela said, her eyes wide. "Isn't that what we do?" and she headed for their park with her bag of day-old sourdough and a cheery cheese croissant she'd sprung for. They had an hour until classes, one of those things Lucy would never know about them. Lucy didn't listen to stories. They did.

Beautiful purple Thursday, with the storm clouds hanging low overhead and the air an electric promise of thunderstorms. Tory was wearing new boots that threatened to make her taller, and Trent sported a Saran-wrapped wrist where a phoenix sprang forth and burned brightly. Angela and Matt slouched behind them, the four making their way to the bread store.

And, "What do you think?" Louise asked, nodding in the direction of the incipient storm and they nodded and affirmed and bought extra carbohydrates because the day was dark and their bodies didn't like it even if their minds did. Louise tucked some chocolate chip scones in and waved away the charge and the four went back the way they'd come, the way they always came, but lightning broke overhead, so close they could hear the sizzle and taste it on the back of their tongues and the hair on the back of their necks stood up. Rain began to fall, straight down, no nonsense rain, and Trent spotted it first, spotted the door in otherwise unbroken expanse of wall, and said, "Come on." Before anyone could ask if they were trespassing or mightn't the door be locked, they were inside.

Dark. Dark with gleams here and there, as if low light from unimagined windows were picking out shiny objects, and then lightning broke overhead again and contrary to logic, the lights went *on*.

"What the *fuck*?" Tory said and the others nodded. They were standing in a hallway, gray as the outside world, lit by low buzzing fluorescents and tinged purple as the storm clouds. Matt stood rubbing his arms. Despite the storm the fall day outside wasn't cold. It was colder inside.

"Where are we?" Angela asked, looking at Trent.

"I don't know. I just opened the door." He shrugged, sending matching archetypes on his shoulders skyward – angel on one shoulder, demon on the other.

Tory, staring around them, pointed. "This way," she said.

"This way what?" Matt asked and Tory shrugged.

"Dunno. It says 'this way,'" and she pointed at the red arrow on the wall, pointing the only way the corridor led. *This way.*

"This way to the exhibit," Angela read.

"What exhibit?" Matt asked.

"*The* exhibit," Angela answered and nodded at the sign as they passed it.

"It's friggin' cold in here," Tory said and the hall jogged right, ran ten feet farther, and dropped them abruptly into the exhibit.

The four of them stood silent for a moment, staring around them, squinting in the dimness and trying to make out just exactly what they were looking at.

"What *are* those?" Matt asked at the same time Angela said, "Are those coffins?" and Tory said briefly, "Yuck!"

It was Trent who ventured down the three stairs into the main arena and first approached the displays. Spread over an enormous room, there were three rows of them heading back into the gloom where presumably a back wall stopped the exhibit. Each row, neatly laid out, contained eight coffins of sorts, glass, and upright, shadowy figures within, and beside the coffin, flanking it, shelves of what looked like random items left behind by somebody in the throes of spring cleaning.

Trent, first, not moving to the closest coffin but to the one off to the left and over to the third row, walking slowly but purposely, the way someone might walk into a doctor's office for a particularly unpleasant treatment. Matt and Angela didn't move but Tory walked as far as the railing and braced her arms against it, as if resisting being drawn down as Trent had.

"Listen to this," Trent said, and began to read. Angela made a small movement, as if to stop him, but Trent was turned slightly away from them, reading the card on the front of the coffin, and didn't see. "Davis Little," he read, his hands moving unconsciously, as if directing his words. He paused to stare through the glass at the face inside the coffin, but the glass was cloudy and dark. "Born 1949."

"Who's Davis Little?" Matt asked. His voice echoed back off the coffins. Angela looked at him like she'd prefer he shut up.

"This guy, I guess," Trent said, gesturing toward the coffin. The glass no longer seemed as darkly clouded.

"There's someone in there?" Tory asked. From their perch they could see five rows back before the coffins blended together from their point of view. "There's someone in each?" Her voice dropped, nervous.

"Listen to this," Trent said again. He had moved slightly to the side of

Davis Little and was reading from the plaque. "By the time he was seven years old, he'd burned down his parents' house," Trent said, skimming down the card. "And then – "

"Who's that?" Matt asked, pointing past Trent farther back into the arena of coffins. Angela and Tory followed his pointing finger. Movement through the rows.

"Hey!" Angela called. "*Hey!* We're not trespassing. It's just that it's raining outside and ..."

"There's no one there," Tory said. Her voice was pissed off. "Let's get the fuck out of here." She rubbed her arms and looked around, the bag of pastries in her hand rattling against her skin. No one answered her, though, and after a moment Trent started reading again.

"Nobody ever proved anything but people's pets disappeared in every neighborhood he lived in."

"Gross," Tory said.

"What's all the stuff on the shelves?" Matt asked. None of them seemed inclined to go as close to the coffins as Trent had.

Trent moved over to stand in front of the shelving. "It's just *stuff*," he said, and then, "wait, there's labels." He was quiet for a second. Something somewhere in the gloom settled, a deep crunch of timbers and beams, and they all jumped. "Oh, hey," Trent said. He turned around and held a high heeled pump in his hands. "See this? It's Mrs. Davis's."

"His wife?" Matt asked.

"His mother." Trent held the shoe, moved back in front of the plaque. "It says…" Silence. Angela fidgeted. Tory's bag crackled as she turned back toward the door, out of sight behind them.

"He killed her," Trent said quietly. When he spoke something rippled across the room and was gone before any of them saw it. On the arena floor, Trent turned suddenly and put his hands on the coffin glass, leaning inward until his nose was almost touching.

"Hey!" Matt yelled, jolting forward. Tory put out a hand to stop him, but Matt was too far away from her, on the steps and moving into the rows of upright glass coffins. Angela moved closer to Tory.

"Where's he going?"

Because Matt was moving away from where Trent stood, hands pressed against the glass, was moving past Trent an down the aisle between the rows and when they looked at Trent again, he seemed completely absorbed, staring into the glass coffin with the rapt attention he usually reserved for his online quests. Something inside the coffin glowed red.

"They shouldn't be down there," Angela said, her voice low. She looked around after speaking, as if looking for anyone who might have heard her.

"I know," Tory said, and climbed over the rail and dropped to the arena floor.

"Don't!" Angela said sharply.

Tory's boots clattered as she hit. "I'll bring Matt back before he gets lost. You just watch Trent," she said, and that was simple enough, because he wasn't moving. Angela reached out anyway, wanting to stop Tory the way Tory'd wanted to stop Matt when he'd gone after Trent. Trent was still standing bewitched in front of Davis Little's coffin even as Tory passed him and disappeared into the gloom of the museum floor. Museum. That was it, not arena, but museum. Angela stopped watching Tory, started to turn back to watch Trent, and found herself instead looking at one of the coffins, a few rows back and to the right of where Trent stood, and she started to call out but only ended up making a kind of choked clicking noise and nobody answered her.

The stairs under her feet seemed to rock a little as thunder exploded again outside and the lights in the museum went off.

She didn't know how she'd gotten there, or even where *there* was but someone nearby seemed to be whispering, whispering, whispering. Angela turned around and around but nothing changed in her perspective. Three was blue sky overhead, with only a hint of storm clouds off in the distance. Corn grew up around her and she was standing in it, a couple rows back from the edge of the field, a house in sight at the edge. She'd never been in a corn field in her life.

Hello? she thought but she didn't speak. Something was nearby. Something she didn't want to have find her. So she stood still, and standing still hurt. Her entire body ached, as if she'd been beaten.

Like you'd know, Angela thought. Her parents had never done anything remotely physical like beating her. Everything from them had been … perfect. The perfect bedroom. The perfect house. Allowed the perfect hours to play, to stay up. And everything else was ignored. She was ignored. So how come she knew what it felt like to be beaten? Her back was fiery. And the voice just kept whispering and whispering and she couldn't hear it closely so she set off to find it, moving cautiously on sore feet, deeper into the corn, away from the house.

"I'm coming," she said finally, her hands up to push against the corn that grew tighter and tighter and at her words the corn opened up and fell away and there in the clearing was the house again.

"Great, I've been going in circles," Angela said, but she knew it wasn't true.

"This way," the voice whispered, and she was lying in a bed, a tiny bed, a tiny girl, and she could hear her mother's voice. "She has to learn, George. The barn is dangerous. I've told her and told her – "

...and her father, gentle – useless! "I understand, honey, but sometimes you're a little harsh – "

--their voices in the night, arguing. The voice, the whispering being, suck Angela's own fingers in her own ears and she lay, her body sore, her mind a starry blank, thinking of the future.

And –

"This way," the voice said and she was standing and watching as mother tumbled down and down from the loft, the fall had to be enough to kill her and if it wasn't, there were cleverly placed pitch forks waiting and then it was just her and daddy, but he never forgave her, long slow life when he made her stay. Otherwise, he'd tell. Otherwise, she'd go to jail, to the electric chair, killed her own mother at the age of ten. Watching as her father aged and punishment transferred from him to her, her punishments growing more inventive, more effective. Waiting, watching, cataloging, and when he died, she found a position in the paper, someone advertising for a companion, and finally she left the farm, headed into town to assist the dying.

Matt ran. Behind him he heard Angela and Tory, the two of them shouting, and then silence, suddenly, as he drew near the coffin, one of the eight in the row, no different from the others, the shelf beside it loaded with the same collection of indefinable stuff. As if told to, he stopped and put his hands on the glass, trying to see in. Visions danced and swirled. Inside the coffin looked like a steam room. Matt brought his hand up as if he could wipe the mist away from the outside. Inside something mirrored his movement. The mist brushed away. Matt saw into the coffin and fell and fell and fell.

Glorious fall day. Thunderstorms swept through during the night and washed away the grime. The city sparkled around him as he made his way to the restaurant. Meeting Cass. They'd sit, have coffee. He'd broken up with Laurie for her. Broken up with Amy. Of course, those relationships had been growing old, had been beginning to wear. He checked his clothes before he entered the café. He hadn't had time to change. Grinned at his reflection in the smoked glass café doors. Grinned at Cass sitting in one of the sunny booths, smiling at him, waiting for him. His steps quickened and he sat down next to her rather than across, put his hands over hers in the sunlight and leaned in to give her a kiss. Sunlight on his nails picked out flecks of blood and he grinned, barely able to contain his joy. Broke up with Laurie. With Amy. Laurie had cried and cried, begging, hadn't wanted him to sever the relationship. She'd cried for nearly an hour before giving in, realizing it was over. Amy had screamed and fought back but in the end, although leaving her had been quicker, it had been more satisfying. Her screams. Her pleading. Ultimately, her tears. She must have really loved him. lost her heart over him. He surfaced from his thoughts and grinned again, sucking Cass in with his eyes. Perfect. Young and blond and happy. Beautiful. They'd be so happy together. Until they weren't. And then the relationship would have to end. He'd have to break up with her. His smile faltered, then returned. All good things come to an end. He smiled at her in the sunlight and they ordered ice cream.

Matt thought he was screaming but no one came. He thought his friends were here somewhere and he thought he was screaming, but no one came. He shoved himself away from the coffin, but the feel of the glass stayed on his hands, like oil or gel or a thick lotion he couldn't quite rub off.

Tory didn't touch the coffin. Somewhere else in the museum she heard Matt say something and she thought about calling out. But the memory of someone there, barely seen, nagged her and she remained silent. *We'll be out of here soon enough. Dear god but this place is creepy.* She ran her hands up and down her arms again and noticed she no longer carried the bag from the bread store. Small loss. She looked around for a moment, turned back to the coffin in front of her. *What am I doing here?* and she started to walk away. Not for her, thank you very much, not staring into someone's coffin whether it's glass or not. But just before she would have headed back up the aisle to find and collect her friends and get the hell out of Dodge, rain or no rain, something caught her eye. Something plain and ordinary, rather like the high-heeled pump Trent had held up earlier.

A shoe. She reached for it before she gave it any thought and grabbed it – a size eight shoe, office wear, a woman's, no big deal, but it seemed a little – and in that instant she was there.

***

Dark parking lot. Smell of ozone from the rain and lightning. Purple sodium lights tingeing the rain. It all felt unreal that day – second day on the job, legal secretary, and already she hated the boss, how long would she last this time? Her friend Jess temped and maybe that was the way to go, up and out of there as soon as it got conflicted. Yeah, she'd call Jess. Give it a little while here, but –

Her key scraped the lock. She jumped at the thunder, stabbed at the door again and hands, big hands, over her nose and mouth, one over her throat hard and her breath choked off and a leg wrapped around hers, and she felt her left knee torque, struggled, and felt him rip the car door open before he shoved her inside and climbed in after her.

Not enough room in the front seat for both of them, it was a VW bug, someone would notice, but no one did, and it seemed like she left her body, left herself, and the pain kept dragging her back. Pain in her throat, her face, her eyes, in her legs and back and radiating through her core and worse when he pulled out the knife and got inventive. But it was the screaming that kept her anchored there, in the moment, in herself. The screaming that didn't sound like hers, that she thought she'd never forget.

Tory surfaced, panicked, like she was drowning though she stood in a dry room with the rain beating outside. She backed away from the coffin, from the shelves, looked down to find she still held the shoe and now the stains on the leather looked like blood. She flung it, convulsively, and turned and ran into the rows of coffins, desperate to find the others and get out.

The screaming followed her.

Trent surfaced when Tory shook him. she was taller than him by a head. He bobbed back and forth in her grip while confused images sped by, something about a knife and a wife and teaching someone a lesson. Something about what real life was and wasn't and a black high-heeled shoe and cheating and then all the others, cheaters all – it fell away and the others were there and he said, "Let's get out of here."

Outside the rain had turned to downpour. One at a time they looked back before they left the street. But they couldn't see the doorway through the rain.

By unspoken agreement they took to walking an alternate route to the bread store on Thursdays but after three weeks fall gave way to winter and freezing rains and they abandoned the store for the year and took to gathering on campus in the Cafeteria of Doom. But they were falling away from each other and by spring they weren't gathering at all but planning for their futures. Futures they hadn't imagined, but things change; they always change.

Trent bought a knife.

Tory bought a dog and listened to music whenever she could. When there was no music, she often sat with her hands over her ears.

Matt began dating, serial dating, judging his relationships harshly and mapping out timelines, when they would begin. When they would End.

Angela got a job in an old folks' home.

The bread store went out of business, Louise going to work in a nonprofit agency and Lucy running through a string of jobs.

The museum continued to open on rainy days, when the light was low and the wind high and people were most likely to grab the unlocked door, and enter.

Jennifer Rachel Baumer lives, writes, runs and procrastinates in the Northern Nevada desert where she lives with her husband and cats in the rural North Valleys, surrounded by jackrabbits, cottontails, coyotes and quail… and possibly ghosts.

Her work can be found in genre magazines and anthologies, both virtual and print, and in the previous collection The Last Oracle & Other Ghostly Tales, available through Amazon.
She also maintains a rather hit or miss blog at
http://jenniferrbaumer.blogspot.com/

A lonely woman in a surreal city haunts her own life.

A new house in a new neighborhood reveals its ghastly secrets.

And the grimoire discovered in the local used bookstore proves to be more than just a curiosity.

How clear is the line between life and death – or between the living and the dead? What happens at the Renaissance Faire when death in the form of the Danse Macabre doesn't pass by?

In this collection of nine haunting tales, award-winning author Jennifer Rachel Baumer reveals the secrets of the dead, and the ghosts of the living.